I0653639

WIND'S
SOLACE

Jeni Burns

WIND'S SOLACE

Media Jam, LLC
15105-D John J. Delaney Drive; #317
Charlotte, NC 28277
www.jeniburns.com

Publisher's Note: This is a work of fiction. Names, characters, places, and incidents are a product of the author's imagination. Locales and public names are sometimes used for atmospheric purposes. Any resemblance to actual people, living or dead, or to businesses, companies, events, institutions, or locales is completely coincidental.

Cover Design: Michelle Fairbanks. Fresh Design
https://mfairbanks.carbonmade.com

Wind's Solace / Jeni Burns. -- 1st ed.
Elemental Love #2
ISBN 978-1-942964-17-9

To Reagan Phillips.
I'm so grateful to have such an amazing
friend in you.

*Random Thought # 19 - When a phone rings
at 3am, it's never for anything good.*

"Ignore the damn phone, I'm almost there," the curvy blonde encouraged over her shoulder as his hips stalled mid-thrust.

If Charlie could have designed his perfect woman, she'd understand his need to answer the phone at three a.m. when a dead body turned up. Unfortunately, Maureen wasn't her. And the one woman who was his perfect match still refused to talk to him.

He ignored her and pulled out, suppressing a groan. Maureen's ill-aimed swat missed his thigh by a hair as he dove for the nightstand.

"Seriously, Chaz," the Earth Elemental whined, and the foundation of his home shook.

"Quit it, Maureen. Work always comes first. You don't like it, leave." He shot her a glare and stabbed the 'talk' button on his cell. "Latham." His voice was thick and had all the charm of a mouth full of gravel. He blamed it on the extra Jack and Coke he'd downed when Maureen showed up uninvited on his doorstep, but truth be told, he hadn't managed a full night's sleep in weeks.

Someone was dumping bodies all over Harmony, White Township, and Hope, New Jersey. If that wasn't bad enough, each body looked more and more like an old friend; a friend Charlie refused to let wander through his mind too often for fear he'd drive to her mother's home and demand to know her whereabouts so he could apologize. Again. Because maybe this time she'd believe him.

"Sorry 'bout the wake-up call, man, but we have a body." The voice of his former partner, Elroy Traver, was too chipper for the early hour. Although, if Charlie remembered right, Roy was finishing off his week of overnights, so his veins would be flush with caffeine thanks to the jumbo cups of dark sludge Roy insisted were coffee but looked more like used motor oil.

Maureen's hand cracked against his bare thigh. "Where?" He glared at her and slid off the bed stumbling over their discarded clothing.

"Jenny Jump."

JENI BURNS

"Again?" *Shit.* This was the second dead body up on Jenny Jump. The nature preserve had gotten more traffic in recent months than it had in the last few years. Some sicko was using the wooded mountainside as their personal dumping ground. Based on the continued resemblance of the deceased to Gracelynn George, Charlie would bet his last shred of dignity the murders had something to do with the secretive community he lived in the midst of. At the thought of her name, his cock twitched. *Damn.* He shook the brunette from his brain.

"Yeah. Pretty sure this is the same guy, but boss man wants you out here to look before the ME arrives. Another fully dressed, soaked woman left on dry land. We need that crazy intuition of yours." Roy's voice derailed the memory train building momentum in Charlie's mind.

"All right. Be there in thirty." Charlie disconnected and flipped on the light switch. The intuition Roy spoke of was more than that, but Charlie could never admit the truth around his human counterparts. Nope. They didn't know Elementals existed—let alone they were their neighbors, friends, and even partners at work. And they sure as hell didn't know they had special gifts. Some more special than others.

"You aren't seriously leaving are you, Chaz?" Maureen raised an eyebrow.

It was time to cut her loose. As it was, she'd already begun getting a little too comfortable. Showing up at all hours like the booty call that wouldn't go away was one thing, but when she tried to interfere with his work, she was going too far.

"How many times do I have to tell you not to call me that?" He growled, pulled off the condom, and dropped it in the waste can. "You gotta go."

"But it's the middle of the night." Her whiny voice grated against his already shot nerves.

He gave the leggy blond a quick once over. "Doesn't matter, sweet cheeks. I've gotta work, and we had an agreement."

"Come on, we've been dating for weeks. Can't I stay?"

Charlie turned in time to catch the look that got him into this mess in the first place. *Damn it.* As much as he enjoyed the way Maureen's body fit with his, their arrangement needed to end. There was no room in his life for a clingy woman — especially not one whose pout made him want to give her a reason to smile until dawn.

"Sorry. It's time to go."

Her pout wavered.

Shit. He turned away from the upset Earth Elemental and located his discarded jeans. As he stuffed his feet into his work boots, something pointed and sharp hit him square in the back; by the feel and the sound it made when the object fell to the floor, he knew Maureen had pitched her spiked heel at him. Instead of turning around to read the look on her face, he opened his mind and allowed her thoughts to hit him full force. *Yep*, she was beyond hurt, she was pissed. Her brain churned at ninety angry miles per second. A dry spell was in his immediate future—he didn't need to be a mind reader to see it coming.

"I get it. We're through. Lock up behind yourself when you leave. I've got to run." He grabbed a soft flannel shirt from the back of his favorite easy chair on his way out of the bedroom. Maureen's thoughts assaulted him like poisoned darts until he closed the imaginary iron gate in his mind to block them out.

A pit stop in the kitchen for emergency caffeine proved a waste of time when his ancient coffee system failed. The sound of things hitting the floor in his bedroom indicated it was time to give up his java quest and get out. He grabbed his keys from the hook by the front door and refused to look back.

The November night air chilled him enough to contemplate going back into his house for a coat—until the flare of lights being turned on in the living room shone through the curtains his mother had hung years ago. He'd rather freeze than face Maureen's wrath. Besides, the last time he'd annoyed her, she'd almost landed his truck in a crater caused by her ground-rattling temper. A temper that was only getting worse as the weeks went on. She'd seemed so sweet and stable when she asked him to meet her at the emergency room after a supernatural crime scene played out in her front yard four weeks ago.

Shit. He was running out of community-approved women to date, and Maureen's big mouth would have him on the least eligible list before dawn. He threw his head back and laughed at the stars. Figured. He lived in a community where true love was destined, and he still couldn't find someone who'd put up with him. Shaking with silent laughter, he slid behind the wheel of his unmarked king cab Dodge. He turned the key until the engine roared to life with the rumble only a Hemi could produce. His high beams reflected off the glass surface of the Delaware River as he drove the backroad that would lead him to another case he'd have to lie and buffalo his way through.

His view of the river ended when the road twisted inland and the water was replaced with trees and farm land. Charlie scratched his early-morning scruff and cranked up the volume when a song by The Killers came on the radio. Fatigue clawed at his eyes and tempted them with dreams of sweet release. Charlie pushed the thoughts from his head, slid the windows open, and embraced the cold air that blasted him as the speedometer needle reached for the sixty-five mark.

The best thing about living in a small town like Harmony was the lack of traffic lights and signs. On a night like this, it would be easy to make the twenty-mile trip in less than twenty minutes. The truck roared down the open roads, cutting through the fog in the low-lying areas and bouncing over the broken bits of pavement last year's harsh winter had left in its wake.

By the time he arrived at the state park, he was wide awake and ready to face the day ahead. A park ranger waved him through the entrance without asking to see his badge. Charlie rolled his eyes. The rangers should know better. Indiscretions like that made it easy for a killer to drop off a dead body. Charlie cracked his neck. Each vertebra popped, and tension he'd ignored since crawling his bare ass out of his warm bed fled.

He parked the truck behind his former partner's Range Rover and unfolded his long limbs in a series of cracks and aches. Hell, he was getting too old for this shit. Not even thirty, his body was done taking the regular beatings he put it through for his job with the state patrol. Being a detective seemed like a great idea, considering his Fate-given gift, but working with humans added an unexpected layer of complication. Telepathy sucked as an advantage, since he was sworn to keep the Elemental Community a secret. His job was a constant tight-rope act of dodging and weaving, while trying to get the guilty to confess and find the proof to keep the innocent free. Although, if all went according to plan, he'd soon be able to turn in his badge, hang up his holster, and make his own hours with a coffee machine that actually worked as designed.

He dug in the glove box for his flashlight and followed the sound of people and glow of light through the trees until he found the dump site. The deceased was female, tall, late twenties, with long brown hair. Duct tape with three *X's* drawn in marker were placed where her eyes and mouth would be—not unlike the last victim found in almost the same spot a few weeks ago. Charlie knelt beside her, gloved his hands, and brushed hair from her face. With the tape in place, he had no point of reference for identifying her, other than she looked like a younger version of Sophie George, the Elemental Community's healer.

He raised the woman's right hand and the curl of blank ink on the underside of her wrist caught his attention. He moved closer and shined his flashlight beam on her pale skin to better inspect the tattoo. *Shit.* A simple black script-style "M" decorated her skin. Warning bells rang in his head. *Double shit.* Which wrist did Sophie's daughter have a similar tattoo on? He clicked the light off and rolled back onto his heels, rifling through his catalog of memories to when he'd first seen the inked Scorpio insignia on Gracelynn's slender arm.

"Where's the ME? We need to get this tape off her face. There's a chance I know the victim." Charlie swung around and came chest to face with Elroy. The portly man Charlie'd come to trust unclipped his walkie from his belt and barked at the dispatch officer on the other end of the line.

"ME's fifteen out," came the crackled reply.

"Ten-four," Roy answered before motioning Charlie away from the throng of people surrounding the drop site. "Who's the woman?"

Charlie pushed his hand through his way-beyond-being-standard-police-issue mop of unruly hair. "I'm not sure until I see the rest of her."

"But you think you know her?" Roy prodded.

"Well, I think she might be someone I grew up with. The hair, height, and tattoo are all similar to Gracelynn George."

"Isn't she the one who went crazy and painted that mailbox hot pink?" Roy circled his index finger around his ear in a 'cuckoo' motion.

The abruptness of the question coupled with the rudeness of the hand gesture put the stiffness back in Charlie's neck. Elroy wasn't wrong. Grae's breakdown around her thirteenth birthday rivaled most newsworthy events in the small New Jersey town. But the facts surrounding her episode weren't anyone's business—especially not a human's. They'd never understand the stress of being a thirteen-year-old Elemental coming into their gifts—or not coming into them, as her case had been. Charlie shot Roy a glare. "She had depression, man. She didn't go crazy." After all these years, Charlie still found himself defending the girl he'd spent way too much time thinking about. Hell, if he took a minute to be completely honest with himself, he thought about Gracelynn George more than any pure-blood should think of an un-fated half-blood by the community's standards. The fact his heart fluttered when he thought of her only made it worse.

"I didn't mean anything by it, man. I just heard the stories," Roy clarified as he dug the toe of his work-issued boot into the ground.

Charlie shrugged off the apology. "No worries." At the confused look on Roy's face, he added, "Our parents were friends, so I knew her." Sure, it was true his parents and Sophie George had been friends, but Grae had meant much more to him. Time and time again, he'd attempted to move past her, but no one else made him want to settle down and give the whole happily-ever-after a real shot.

"And you think she might be our Jane Doe?"

Roy interrupted his stream of consciousness. "Maybe. The tattoo..." He stopped himself shy of saying he'd spent time twirling his tongue over the pattern back in high school, hoping she'd be his fated one. "I think she had a similar one. It could be her, but last I heard, she wasn't in town." The thought of Grae safe and sound in North Carolina offered him some peace of mind.

"Gotcha. Want to wait with the body?" Roy nodded his head toward where other officers were setting up high-powered lighting equipment in preparation for the ME's arrival. "Or you want to hang over there?"

"Nah. Until there's a report from the ME, there isn't much I can do. I think I'll head home and get some more shut-eye."

"All right. We still on for beers after work tonight?" Roy asked.

"Sure thing. Just give me a heads-up after the ME finishes with the body."

"You got it." Roy waved a mock salute in his direction before adding, "And, Charlie, if it is the George woman, I'll call you ay-sap."

"Thanks, Roy." Charlie thumped Roy on the back and trudged back to his truck. If there was a killer on the loose who was targeting women who looked like one of his community's most well-known half-breeds, he wasn't sure the police department was ready for the task ahead. *Collateral damage* and *human* were synonymous during battles within the supernatural community.

Blood pounded in his ears as he refused to believe the woman with the haunting hazel eyes no longer walked this earth. He needed a breather. One last look at the crime scene cemented his resolve. If Grae was alive, he'd find a way to make her forgive him—maybe then he'd sleep better at night.

∽

Charlie turned onto Shades of Death Road and his situation hit him full force. He couldn't go home. With his luck, Maureen's temper had left only the foundation of his house intact. He steered his truck toward Belvidere and drove. A groan slipped from his lips. He should've known better before getting involved with her—a damn Earth Elemental. What was wrong with him? He knew Maureen went out of her way to avoid getting stuck with a fated match and preferred dating humans, but she'd been so sad and vulnerable when she'd suggested grabbing dinner, he'd agreed without thinking.

Now he'd pay the price for his impetuousness. Hell, his house would pay if she stewed over his early morning departure and flippant breakup. He shifted into park at the first stop sign and wrestled his cell phone from his back pocket. It was almost four-thirty. There was a chance Declan Price would wake soon, since he saw little value in wasting time on frivolous activities like sleep. Charlie pressed Dec's speed dial number and shifted back into drive.

"Yo?"

"Dec, it's Charlie. You up?"

"I am now."

The grumpiness in Declan's voice didn't go unnoticed. "Good. I'm on my way." Charlie switched the blinker from left to right and headed toward the downtown area of Belvidere.

"To where?"

"Your place. It's been a hell of a morning already, and my coffee pot's on the fritz again."

"So you're waking me up at"—a muffled shuffling of covers sounded over the speaker—"*four-twenty-eight in the morning*? Are you kidding me! You call me this early and want me to make you coffee? Damn it, Charlie. If, you were a chick, I'd expect a reward for this shit."

Charlie steered around the curves of the backroads leading toward Main Street and smiled. Dec's grumpiness would be easy to appease. "I get it, man. How about I buy your beers tonight? We're meeting Roy."

"Whatever."

Charlie heard him rustling around.

"The door's unlocked, just let yourself in." Dec's voice dropped to a whisper.

"You have company?" Charlie tried to keep the surprise out of his voice but it seeped in loud and clear anyway.

"Elms and Simon are crashing here."

That was odd. Elms was Dec's cousin and the Community's apprentice healer. She and her new husband, tech genius Simon Foster, had been staying at the George place while Sophie was out of town for some reason or another. Charlie'd heard the rumors that Sophie'd gone to North Carolina to visit with Grae, but he didn't put stock in rumors.

"Sophie's back and it was a little crowded for the newlyweds. Especially since Gracie came with her."

Charlie's stomach took a nosedive.

Shit.

2

Random Thought # 56 - Enough beer can cure just about anything — except a broken heart. That requires whiskey, and lots of it

Charlie let himself into Declan's Victorian-mansion-turned-apartment and shucked his boots in the foyer. The old place still had all the charm that belonged in a house built in the late 1800's, but also the modern feel of an updated three-story house converted into two apartments. Declan's unit began on the second floor and navigating the winding wooden stairs in the dark was harder than Charlie imagined.

A small antique table lamp illuminated the cluttered living room with a soft glow.

"Full octane?" Declan spoke in an exaggerated whisper from the galley kitchen.

"Hell yeah. I'll be running on this all day," Charlie answered as he joined his friend. He perched on the counter and watched Dec fill the high-tech coffee machine. Declan's glasses sat askew on his face in happy conjunction with his tousled, dirty-blond, bed-head locks, which stuck out at angles not yet discovered in standard geometry. "Sorry to get you up so early. I couldn't go back to my place."

"Some pretty little thing pouting?" Dec's eyebrows waggled with the question, adding to the comedic look he shot Charlie's way.

"Does Maureen count?"

Declan's face brightened and a guffaw broke through his restrained I've-got-guests-sleeping volume. "Shit! You're in the doghouse, man. I hear Maureen holds a grudge. Plus, didn't she kill her last boy-toy?"

"Not exactly." Charlie had kept the details of Maureen's ex quiet. Partly out of habit because of his job, and partly because he still couldn't wrap his mind around what he'd seen the night Dax Barren died.

The coffee maker beeped, signaling the end of its cycle.

"Grab mugs from the cabinet to your right, will ya?"

Charlie slid off the counter and opened the cherry cabinet door. Unlike the mismatched set of dishes he'd collected over the years, Dec had a full set of eight navy blue mugs. Between Dec's mom and his cousin, he lived a bachelor's life, but kept all the benefits of having a woman to help decorate and organize his home.

Shaking his head, Charlie grabbed the two mugs closest to the edge of the shelf and passed them to his friend. "I should warn you there's a chance Maureen'll call you later to bitch."

"Why? What'd you do this time?"

Charlie sipped the hot, black, caffeinated goodness and considered how to break the news to his friend. Declan and Maureen had dated years ago, before they were of age to mate, and their time together ended on good enough terms that the two had remained friends. Hence Maureen being in Charlie's orbit enough for him to feel bad when her last boyfriend died on her front lawn. One of the drawbacks to small town living, he supposed. Eventually, everyone knew everyone else, and the singles started pairing off.

It made perfect sense though, him and Maureen. Neither was hell-bent on finding their fated mate. Despite the cardinal rule of not dating outside your element within the community, both Charlie and Maureen preferred the appeal of someone outside their community entirely, which granted them rule-breaker status for life. Too bad he'd realized she was getting a little too comfortable with their agreeable arrangement. But with Declan's cousin, Elms, granted the community's blessing to mate a Fire in spite of her being a Wind, Declan was surely going to get an earful if Charlie knew Maureen at all.

"I might've kicked her out of bed this morning when I got called to a crime scene." Charlie ducked his head and slid back onto the countertop.

WIND'S SOLACE

"I thought you two had a no sleep-overs poli-
cy?" Declan stirred cream and sugar into his coffee
mug before turning his hundred-watt glare in
Charlie's direction.

"Yeah, me too. Apparently, she thinks something's changed." Charlie hopped off the counter
and retreated to the living room couch, knowing it
was close enough to the bedrooms that Dec would
keep his voice down.

"Fuck. Elms sure has stirred up a shitstorm of
trouble by mating with Simon." Dec nodded toward the nearest closed bedroom door. "But I
can't help kinda liking the guy. He's sharp and
really knows his stuff. He even offered to help design some all-encompassing data software. Was
thinking of running it by you tonight."

Declan settled into a recliner that didn't match
a single other piece of furniture in the room. Charlie figured it was the only piece in the whole
apartment Dec fought his mother on. A smile tickled his lips.

Charlie's smile faded as abruptly as it occurred.
"Besides a program you could probably produce,
what else can he bring to the business?"

Declan leaned forward to the point of almost
tipping the recliner on its base and lowered his
voice. "How about millions? We wouldn't need the
investment group in New York if we took Simon
on." Dec's left eyebrow rose until it got lost in the
mop of hair hanging over his forehead.

A low whistle escaped Charlie's lips. "And he's
willing to let us run the day to day?"

Dec shrugged the question off. "Pretty much."

"Hmm. Let's schedule a meeting with him, and I'll dig around to make sure his intentions are what we're expecting."

"Whatever you want," Declan agreed. "So...when can you leave the force?" He relaxed into his seat and sipped his coffee.

"Not until we get the sick bastard who keeps leaving dead bodies out at Jenny Jump."

"There's another one?"

"Yeah, and this one looks a lot like Gracelynn George." Mentioning her by name sent a lead balloon of dread straight to the depths of his soul.

"Oh, shit. Does Sophie know?" Coffee sloshed over the edge of Dec's mug and splashed onto his Red Baron Snoopy sleep pants.

"Not yet. The ME needs to do their thing and confirm it, but the DB has a tattoo like one I remember seeing on her." Charlie watched his friend wave a hand over the saturated fabric of his pants in a weak attempt to dry the material. When that failed, Dec called up his Wind element until a light breeze morphed out of the air around them.

"*Wow.* Sophie'll be devastated if it's her daughter, won't she? Just last night, Elms told me at dinner that Sophie and Gracie have only recently reconnected. I heard she came back because she wanted to talk to her mom. Something about her gifts. Or... maybe it had to do with the healing studio. Elms said she's concerned Gracie might be joining them at the clinic," Declan mused while the constant stream of air dried the spilled coffee.

"That's what the grapevine says, although I find it hard to believe Gracelynn George would ever come back to Harmony just for her mom's advice." Charlie borrowed from Dec's excess Wind, calling his own Wind nature to gently swirl over the caffeinated lava in his mug until it was room temperature.

"Why not? Don't all women come around to their mom's way of thinking by the time they're in their twenties?" Apparently satisfied with his air dry, Declan sipped at the remaining contents of his mug.

"Not sure. But Gracelynn built up some pretty strong resentment over the years. Hell, I remember one night her swearing off Elementals and all of Harmony. She said once she got out of here, she'd never come back." Charlie gulped his coffee down in two big swallows and set the mug on the floor beside his feet.

Declan shot from his seat and snatched up the empty mug before there was a chance for a ring to stain the floor. "You remember all that?" Dec's eyebrows made their journey north again. "Was there something between you two?" He whisper-yelled as he retreated to the kitchen to refill their mugs.

"Nah." Charlie bit off the word and cut his friend an ice-laden glare.

"Uh huh," Dec chided over his shoulder from the kitchen. "You remember the girl's tattoo and her solemn pledge disavowing the community, but there was nothing between you. Sure." Sarcasm dripped from his words as he returned with only one steaming mug and handed it to Charlie. "Look, we both know you'll throw yourself into this case like you did with all your others. You'll complain and bitch that the humans don't appreciate you, and moan that you could do this sooooo much easier if you were all on your own, but you

won't quit. And before this case closes, there will
be another. And another. And another. You need
to decide if you really want in on the new business. I'm tired of working for an asshole who
makes me punch a timecard and fix all his issues
because he's a two-bit programmer with absolutely
no motivation. I'm so fed up with it, I might've
already sent him a '*Dear John, take this job and
suck it*' email." Dec flopped back into the recliner
and rocked it.

"No way. I thought you weren't ready to quit
until we got funding." Charlie set his drink on top
of a magazine on the coffee table and watched his
friend for any signs of deception, but nothing
popped. "Don't make me go digging around in
your head for the info, Dec," he warned, as the
iron gate in his brain began to creak open.

"I know I said I wanted your okay on Simon,
but really, he's exactly what we need. And he's
one hell of a programmer," he added before Charlie could argue. "I've tried breaking every piece of
software he's developed, and it hasn't been easy.
Sometimes it's downright impossible. That's the
Goddess-honest truth, so leave my brain alone."

"You're what? Hacking your new partner?"
Charlie's bitter tone landed him one of Dec's disapproving stares square at his chest.

"I needed to know how good he was. And it
turns out, he's good. Really good. Maybe even better than me." Dec's gaze fell to the floor as he absently mussed his hair.

"When are we starting this?"

"*I'm* starting the business by month's end. I've
already begun filling out the paperwork, and Simon's drawing up a partnership agreement. Plus,

he was okay with signing Colin on as our tracker, which given the Elms and Colin love triangle thing, I thought was pretty decent of him."

Colin DeGrasse was a Wind with the ability to shift into any form he chose and a good friend of the group. If Declan had already gotten Simon's agreement in bringing Colin on board, things were moving faster than Charlie had thought.

"So when do you need me to start?"

"Look, Charlie...there will always be a spot for you when you are ready to leave the force. We both know the community wants you to stay on with the PD because of your gift. That, plus your innate sense of duty, while admirable, is what keeps you going back."

"What are you saying Dec?"

"I'm saying the job will be here when you're ready for it, but I might need to hire someone else until then. No pressure. 'Kay?"

"Sure." Charlie nodded on autopilot as the word left his mouth, but his brain screamed at him to make a statement. To commit to a date, a timeframe—heck, a year—that would ensure his departure from the human-run police force. But the louder his brain screamed, the more his heart hardened. His heart was the lucky bastard that knew his friend was right. The community needed him to take his abilities and apply them to the human police force. Having an Elemental inside a government agency shielded the whole community from prying human eyes, as well as provided important information to the community elders to ensure their continued safety. At the mere mention of leaving the force years ago, he'd been told in no uncertain terms it wasn't in the best interests of the community. Forget his plans and goals. His life belonged to other people.

An hour later, Charlie sat glued to the same spot on Declan's sofa. His second cup of coffee remained untouched on the magazine-turned-coaster, and his friend snored from his seat on the recliner. Thoughts he wanted to escape chased him with wild abandon until he ended up in the same place he'd started. There was no getting around it. Not really, anyway. As much as he despised being used by the community to *manage* the humans, he also hated the idea of hiding himself—a telepathic bear in a baby's clothing, so to speak. Dead women were turning up, and he refused to walk away. His abilities alone ensured the right asshole paid for the horrible crimes. Even though he hated the circumstances that landed him this responsibility-laden role, he couldn't ignore innocent women dying in his town. The worst part of it all? They died on sacred land. Land his ancestors long believed held the key to their gifts. Land no human walked on without feeling the presence of spirits. Land so sacred, community elders concocted stories of murderous ghosts to keep people away.

No. He couldn't turn his back on the history—on the dead. Hell, he'd already made the mistake of turning his back on Gracelynn once, and if she was the DB in the woods, he'd do everything in his power to bring her killer to justice. It was the least he could do for her after all they'd been through together.

The squeak of old hinges pulled him from his thoughts. The door to the guest room opened and Dec's cousin peered around the edge.

"Charles."

A single word said it all. Elms still disapproved of his actions from a few months back. Her mate and half the community probably shared her sentiment.

"Elma." He rarely called her by her given name, but until she stopped glaring at him and calling him Charles, it was best to act professional.

"I thought I heard voices earlier. Is everything okay?" Elms' long red hair was plastered, lifeless and limp, to her face, and her blue eyes were shadowed by puffy bags beneath them, her usual petite frame looked oddly out of proportion.

Before Charlie could formulate a response, her eyes widened, her hands flew to cover her mouth, and her feet moved like a cartoon character's on hyper speed. She tore through the apartment, crashing through the half-closed bathroom door, and noises he knew all too well—thanks to his affinity for one-night stands with inebriated women—bounced off the walls. He waited a beat to see if Elms would call out, but when he heard nothing except the soft sound of tears, his body moved of its own accord.

He unfolded his long limbs and crossed the apartment to the open bathroom door in a breath. Elms clung to the porcelain throne's cold rim, heaving, while tears streamed down her face.

He'd trained for this moment. He grabbed two clean towels from the linen cabinet, wet and wrung one, then wrapped it around the back of her neck. When the water warmed, he repeated the motions with a second towel then knelt beside her to wipe the evidence of her episode from her face in gentle, even strokes.

When the heaving stopped, Elms slid to the floor, relief evident in her every movement. "You didn't have to do that."

"I know."

"Thank you." She turned the full force of her big blue eyes on him.

"Am I forgiven?" The worlds left his lips without him considering the blow-back, and when Elms hesitated before answering, he wished he could suck them back in.

"Yes," she finally agreed. "But don't think you can go around arresting my sister-in-law without me getting upset about it." She presented him with a pointed look that pierced his heart.

"I didn't arrest her. I just threatened to." He paused to make sure she was really paying attention, "She tried to *kill* you." He hoped the emphasis would land its intended strike in his favor, but by the look on her green-around-the-gills face, he doubted it achieved his desired result.

"Pssh. It was basically my fault. Siobhan was only trying to protect Simon, and if I can forgive her, you should too." She cocked her head to the side as if waiting for a rebuke.

All out of fight, he nodded. Was it a nod of agreement? Nope. Did Elms need to know that? No way. Would it get him out of trouble with his captain if he ever learned Charlie let an attempted murderer walk away? Hell, no. He rubbed his throbbing temple with one hand and offered Elms his other.

"Thanks." She clutched it and rose to her feet. "Pregnancy is a lot tougher than I ever thought."

The world froze as her words sank in. The news shouldn't surprise him, since Elms was a newly-mated Elemental and her husband, Simon, doted on her left and right. But Simon being a Fire, and Elms a Wind, made the likelihood of a successful pregnancy small. It had been a freak occurrence when Fate paired two supposedly incompatible members of the community, but a baby made it a whole 'nother thing. A permanent thing. A newly-blended member of their community was growing right inside this petite Wind.

He stood staring at Elms and her protruding belly with a mixture of admiration and condolence. Little whips of baby fine thoughts brushed at the iron gate in his head. Unlike most thoughts, these spoke of mysterious things. Places he couldn't understand or imagine. An existence he dared not dream. One thought swirled around the barrier of his brain and seeped through loud and clear.

Save her. Her fate is twined with ours. Without her, neither you, nor I, will exist.

He dropped Elms' hand, choked on bile rising in his throat, and ran from the apartment knowing two things:

Gracelynn wasn't dead yet...and he needed to save   her.

3

Random Thought # 23 - Bars are meat markets the FDA doesn't regulate.

Gracelynn George hated bars. She also hated the now-constant stream of voices in her head; but to deal with one, she had to endure the other. The seemingly flawed rationale was how she found herself in the only bar in all of Harmony, NJ.

She hadn't been legal the last time she set foot in Harmony, so stepping over the threshold of The Outpost wasn't like being transported through time. It was, instead, rather ordinary. She glared around the noisy room and wrinkled her nose against the smell of hops and grease.

Booths lined the outer walls, and tables were strewn about in no apparent order, other than to maximize the number of liquor-buying patrons. A small bandstand stood at one end of the large room, and a mirror-backed bar took up the opposite side. One square area of scuffed flooring was devoid of anything but dancers stepping and shuffling to the melody of a country tune.

The noise collided against her ear drums, rivaling the noise beating against them from inside her skull, and warred until her head threatened to finally explode from it all. Her mother had warned her crowded places could cause the cacophony to get overwhelming. And, as much as it grated her ass to acknowledge her mom was right, there was no denying Sophie George knew her stuff, which meant the bartender here would have the Fate-given gift of knowing exactly which concoction of liquor would cure what ailed her, just like her mom promised.

Determination set in, spurring her into action, and she crossed the width of the establishment until she was close enough to see the defiant lift of her own chin and the fierceness blazing with her eyes from the reflection of the mirror backing the bar. She shook her head, hoping to equalize the warring volumes and remove the intimidating look on her face, then she pulled out a tall stool and sat. Oblivious to the people around her, she buried her nose in the small leather-bound drink menu and tried to block out the thoughts of every person in the room.

She peeked over the top of the menu long enough to locate the owner and head bartender, Eddie. He looked exactly as her mom had described him. Mid-forties, beer belly, thinning brown hair, and the most engaging coal-colored eyes she'd ever seen. As if he could feel her glare boring holes into him, he raised his head in acknowledgment and sauntered her way.

"What'llyuhbehavin'?"

His words were one big mumble of mishmoshed syllables, with no apparent pause in between. With the noise in her brain making thought near impossible, she stared at him and hoped the meaning of his words would come to her out of thin air. When nothing happened, she gave her head a violent shake, a scold of sorts, to quiet some of the intruding voices.

"Ah. Yu'll beneedin' muh 'pecial mix." This time Eddie exaggerated his words to allow for pauses, but he followed his statement with a conspiratorial wink and didn't wait for her answer.

He reached for bottle after bottle, pouring an ounce here, two there, and another from one last brightly colored bottle, into a metal shaker. His hands easily palmed the container and lid. With one more wink, he gave it four hearty shakes. A highball glass appeared like magic from beneath the bar, and he tossed in two sugar cubes, before pouring the liquid. The cubes fizzled, as though annoyed by the intrusion of the alcohol, and sent bubbles racing to the surface. Eddie slid a ripe raspberry around the edge of the glass until it split enough to grab the rim and hold on. He set the glass at her fingertips, smiled, winked again, and wandered back down the bar.

WIND'S SOLACE

The thing about Harmony, it was a curious town with curious people. Most humans never noticed the little oddities the Elementals in town exhibited, but Gracelynn had seemed adept at distinguishing Elementals from humans her entire life, despite not having any Fate-given gifts of her own. The twinkle in the bartender's eye confirmed what her mom had told her—Eddie was an Elemental. Likely, a Water, considering his gift with drinks.

Unlike the pure-blooded Elementals, Gracelynn didn't have what she referred to as *magic*, but her mom oftentimes suggested her ability to pick Elementals out of a crowd might be a low-level gift. While she disagreed, for the better part of the last twelve years, she'd hoped her mom's theory was true. Maybe then she'd be worthy of the community she wanted desperately to join. The noise in the bar notched up as a rowdy group of men jostled through the door. She threw an eye-roll over her shoulder and ground her teeth against the fresh onslaught of thoughts.

Determined to quiet her newly-acquired skill, she wrapped her hand around the still bubbling glass and brought it to her nose. A quick sniff identified nothing beyond the raspberry garnish with a hint of something sweet. The rational part of her said to flag Eddie down and order something familiar. Instead, she raised the glass in silent toast to her reflected image on the other side of the bar. Despite the sugar cubes, the contents were a bitter, fire-breathing, suffocating mixture of hellfire and demon ash. Sputtering, she plunked the glass down and coughed.

JENI BURNS

A swift *thunk* landed hard against her back and surprise jolted her focus from the burn. She swung around, ready to fight, and came face to face with the only person in the world she'd rather have her toenails ripped from her body than lay eyes on— Charlie-fucking-Latham. Oh, this night was destined for the shitter.

She arranged her face into the look she'd perfected because of this guy—part annoyance, part defiance, and all intimidating Jersey Girl. Of course, when she began working on it, he'd been the stupid teenage boy who'd broken her heart for the last time. Now, she'd accrued years of misbehaving boyfriends—hotheaded alpha types and sniveling shorties with God-complexes—allowing her the time it took to further hone the Jersey Girl's *fuck off and die* look.

When she finally met his stare, Charlie's expression wasn't the expected chagrin, or even regret. Instead, relief—coupled with something she couldn't put her finger on—flooded his damn fine face.

Was it happiness? That couldn't be right.

She allowed her eyes to flutter closed and tried to focus on the voices that had been milling around in her head, searching for one that belonged to him, only to find all of them were now suspiciously quiet. She opened her eyes and stared straight into Charlie's cerulean blue irises. They twinkled like sapphires in sunlight, but not a single thought crossed the threshold to her brain. *Shit.* This was the worst time to find a cure for her budding telepathy. She desperately wanted to know what made this man so happy to see her for the first time in over ten years.

4

Random Thought # 9 - A heart doesn't break even. Just ask the guy holding the greater number of pieces.

∿

Charlie stared open-mouthed at the woman who'd haunted his dreams since he'd turned thirteen. Not to mention, she'd nagged his tired brain all day. Thank Goddess Grae was alive and well. True, she was doing her best to kill him with her gorgeous hazel eyes, but thankfully, she didn't have the skill-set for such things. The longer he looked at the womanly shape which had overtaken the tom-boyish figure of his friend, the more her angry thoughts broke through the barrier in his mind. He cursed the soft spot in his heart which allowed her unfiltered access to ooze her way in.

"What the fuck are you smiling about?"

Hearing the f-bomb brought fond memories to the forefront of his mind. He'd forgotten how adorable the brunette beauty looked when she cursed. Her vocabulary suggested old harried sailor, but when curses poured from between her soft pouty lips, the words lost their acidity and gained a decadent sweetness. Possibly he held the opinion because he could still feel those lips on his. Sure, a long time had passed, but they still looked as tempting and kissable as they had back then.

Later, when people asked what overcame him, he'd use the memory of her lips and plead insanity. But that was for the future Charlie to sort out. This was now. And now, he needed to feel that perfect mouth beneath his own.

Kissing her was his first wrong move. Intercepting the hand she swung at his face was the second. But like any guy on the brink of insanity, he went one step further and made the third, and most fatal, of all his mistakes. He held tight to her wrist, kissed her senseless, and pulled as much of her body against his he could, until his brain memorized the way her every curve fit against him.

Good Goddess! She tasted like sugar and berries, fire and passion, sin and seduction. A single kiss felt like a single drop of rain in the dessert. He needed more. Craved it. He thrust his free hand into the heavy mop of thick hair hanging alongside her face and gathered it in his fist.

A gentle tug coaxed a gasp from her. It mingled with his own heated breath in a fevered mating of spirits. He accepted the parting of her lips as an invitation to invade her mouth with his tongue. Somewhere within the soft, warm depths of her body, he lost himself. Heaven couldn't compete with the sensation of surrendering his soul to her.

Until her boney damned knee made swift contact with his groin. Yeah. This was the moment future him would look back on and shake his head with the ability to see exactly where he'd gone wrong. But still, the allure of her called out over the screaming pain in his manhood.

His plan to avoid mating for life like the other saps in the community finally made perfect sense. He was too stupid to produce intelligent offspring, based on his next decision. Fated gifts were meant to be used to accomplish important things, not figure out why a woman who kneed him in the groin still looked like she wanted him to kiss her.

He tore his lips from hers, met her eyes, and probed her with his telepathy. Anger covered hurt. Surprise covered want. And at the very bottom of it all was need. Need he could work with.

He released her hair and wrist but refused to step away. Standing so close, his heart thundered in his chest. Charlie paid no attention to the clatter and chatter of the 'Post. All he saw was her. Grae. The girl he'd loved since his thirteenth birthday when she climbed into his treehouse against his *no girls allowed* rules and handed him a pan of warm brownies.

To hell with the rules. To hell with right and wrong. To hell with what the community would think. Her need spoke to him back then, and it begged his own now. This time, he refused to ignore it.

He grabbed her slender waist and plucked her off the stool, setting her down on heels that were more hooker and hell-raiser than the therapist he'd heard she'd become.

But the Grae he'd known had never been one to conform to the ideals of others. No. She'd been a rule-breaker back in the day, and the outfit she wore tonight was confirmation enough she might still be out to break a few things. Rules. Hearts. Whatever she desired. Her stare bored its way through his thick skull and yanked him back to the here and now. With the here being the bar, and the now being the *kiss my ass and die* look she aimed his way.

"It's been a long time, Grae. I deserved that, but how about you and I go someplace quiet so I can apologize more thoroughly." His voice was low and thick, thanks to the desire streaming through his body, setting him on edge.

"Not on your life. You're lucky I'm not gonna be in town long enough to bother pressing charges, you, you, you..."

Fucker flitted through his mind in her voice.

"Neanderthal," she finally finished aloud on a breath.

"Only around you," he countered. "You've always had that effect on me, you know." His words were truer than the smirk he pasted on his face for her benefit let on.

"Don't." She jerked away and bumped into the stool she'd been perched on. One word said so much. Her nostrils flared and her pupils expanded, until only the golden ring of her iris was visible.

"I'm sorry, Grae. I didn't mean to upset you." He crossed his arms and bit his lip to keep the words he wanted to say from spilling forth.

"Don't give yourself so much credit, Charles. I meant nothing to you years ago, and you sure as hell don't mean anything to me now." She raised her left hand and flashed a delicate ring with a dark center stone sitting in a square border of...diamonds, if the sparkle indicated anything. His dumb luck continued when he realized she wore the ring on her third finger. Of course she did. A woman like Grae wouldn't still be single this late in her twenties.

"I didn't realize." He backed away to put some space between them. "Sorry," he mumbled under his breath. Whatever had come over him still clung to his heart and fogged his brain.

He bumped into someone behind him, and whirled around to find another woman with a disapproving look on her face. Maureen. *Shit.* This night wasn't going to end well. The familiar buzz of his phone vibrating was all he needed in way of a rescue.

He slid the cell from his rear pocket. "Latham," he barked into the handset. Then he shrugged at Maureen and made a bee-line to the quietest place in the bar—the men's room.

"Charlie?"

The woman's voice on the other end of the line sounded familiar, but it just didn't register.

"Yeah, who's this?"

"Charlie, it's Elms. She's dead. Sophie's dead." Her hiccup was the natural punctuation of her phrase.

Time slowed. His pulse tick-tocked a steady rhythm in the tile room, and in the blink of an eye, it all came crashing down on him. "Tell me everything." A growl rumbled in the depths of his chest.

"I just walked in the door. She's dead, Charlie! Did you hear me? Dead!" Hiccups turned to all-out sobs, then the line became a muffled jumble of sniffling and what he could only guess was nose-blowing.

"Are you at Sophie's, Elms?" He burst through the bathroom door, impatience nipping at his heels like the devil chasing him down. "Elms," he yelled above the noise in the bar. "Where the hell are you?"

"Sophie's." The word broke on another sob.

"I'm on my way," he reassured her, pushing through the bar's patrons as he made his way toward Grae. The flash of a thought cut through all the noise in his head with a vengeance. He stopped, slid the phone from his ear, and let the gate in his head slide free.

The thoughts of every person in the building crashed through his mind with the force of a tidal wave. They swirled and churned between friends, his former partner, townies and strangers alike, until he found the one that had made him pause. Malice clung to every nuance of it, sending bile up Charlie's throat. Someone here was drenched in guilt—the stench of it wafted from every corner of the place and choked him. He tried to focus on finding the source, but too many minds were in the mix.

A commotion by the bar broke through his concentration, drawing his gaze to the woman he still didn't regret kissing. The look in her eyes could only be described as terror, but a quick once over of the room didn't show any cause for the crinkle in her brow and frown pulling at her lips. Maybe she'd heard about her mom. That would make sense. Elms probably called Grae before calling him. Decision made without a second thought, he shouldered his way through the crowd, until his fingers brushed her upper arm. She jumped as if she'd been burned and jerked from his grasp until she toppled from the stool.

He pulled her back to her feet, tucked her under his arm, and led her from the bar with a nod at Eddie. By the time they hit the gravel of the parking lot, the voices in his head were quiet again and his first line of defense was securely in place. He steered them toward his truck on autopilot, until her heel made contact with the arch of his boot, and her bony elbow landed in his lower abdomen.

"What the fuck?" He clutched his stomach and took some of his weight off his throbbing foot. *Damn it!* Heels hurt like a sonofabitch. His glare hit its intended target in time to see her to rear back and send a fist flying toward his face. *Shit.* This wasn't what he needed right now. He dropped to the gravel, avoiding her fist, then bounced back to snatch her around the waist and lift her off her feet until she lay over his shoulder. On a different day, this would be the beginning of a thorough fucking in the back of his truck, but not tonight.

"Put me down!"

Her fists pounded on his back and her shoes kicked at his already tender middle, but he didn't break his stride. Instead, he gritted his teeth against the pain and tried to pull his keys from his pocket, growling as they eluded him. She increased both the intensity and frequency of her assault until he itched to land a swift smack against the ripe ass nestled against his cheek, a move he typically reserved for consensual play in the bedroom. His hand stung, the heat of desire rushing to his palm warring with the cold night air. Sighing, he wrestled the keys from his pocket, unlocked the door, and deposited the now-quiet Grae into the passenger seat.

"Buckle up."

"Where are you taking me?" she demanded, her face was flushed in the dome light of the cab, but her eyes were colder than the Antarctic in wintertime.

"To your mom's," he answered, before closing the door and taking enough deep breaths to cool the heat streaking through his veins.

The pink on her cheeks had unraveled his cool by the time he climbed into the driver's seat, because now all he could imagine was a matching pink handprint on her ass.

He was screwed.

5

Random Thought #107 - One's sense of reality really takes a beating in the face of death.

Gracelynn kept quiet when Charlie's truck rumbled to life. The effect of the drink she only got a few sips of was slowly wearing off, and snippets of thoughts danced in her head again, only this time they were images more than words. Images of her spread out in the bed of a truck—this truck, maybe—naked under a moonlit sky, hair splayed around her in a halo. Then, a flash of pink on her cheeks—both on her face and those covered by her skirt—flitted across her mind.

She sucked in an unsteady breath and willed her heart to slow down, but it refused with no apology, and her brain seemed hell-bent on seeing more. She closed her eyes and pressed her hands to them, silently begging whatever common sense she might possess to shut down the stupid gift that allowed her such intimate access to other people's inner monologue. She didn't want to see Charlie's thoughts, even if they were flattering and focused on her, because she knew he would inevitably stray to something else. And, if he was anything like he was back in the day, he'd stray to *someone else* and leave her with more heartache than one woman could stand.

He cleared his throat. The sound bounced around the king cab as if they were deep beneath the earth in their very own secret cavern of solitude. She would kill for some music to help focus her brain elsewhere. A second later, as if he'd plucked the thought straight from her brain, the truck's radio sprang to life with an old song by The Killers. She turned her thoughts to the lyrics, then joined in on the chorus, and the images in her head dissipated with every beat of the music. That song ended and another began. Same group singing into the night. *He must have it on CD or something.* She wished a class in telepathic mastery had been offered with the onset of her gifts, then she could pluck things straight from Charlie's head. Like most things Fate tossed her way, an instruction manual wasn't in the mix.

"Why are you taking me home? I wasn't drunk, I could've driven home when I was ready to leave." She eyed him under the cover of the dark night as the tree-lined road roared by.

Shock played across his features. "I didn't want you driving...under the circumstances."

"What circumstances? I told you I wasn't drunk."

"I know you aren't drunk, Grae," Charlie turned to face her for a brief instant before looking back at the road. "Elms called and told me something's happened to Sophie."

"What? What are you talking about? Mom's home with a patient. That's why I went out."

"I don't have any details, but I thought Elms called you, 'cause you kinda looked a little green there at the bar."

Gracelynn studied the man beside her and tried to dip into the meaning behind his words without getting the barrage of images that had flooded her system, but she was met with resistance.

Even though it'd been close to ten years since she last saw the man, not much had changed. He was still larger than life in every way imaginable, but why would Elms call Charlie if something had happened to *her* mom? It wasn't like he was a healer or anything. If she remembered correctly, he was a detective. She glanced around the truck's interior and confirmed that memory with the extra equipment and buttons she couldn't identify. Her tongue stuck to the roof of her mouth as the answer to her question became apparent. Elms called Charlie *because* he was a detective. *Shit.*

"What's wrong with my mom?" Her whispered question barely broke the surface of her lips.

"Grae, I'm sorry, but I don't know."

"But you're a cop. Elms called you, and you're a cop." The words tumbling from her mouth were a jumble of nonsense, but he still hadn't answered her question. "What happened to my mom?" This time she managed to construct a coherent sentence with the force of a pissed off bronco. Somewhere deep inside, she knew what his answer would be, yet she needed to hear it from him.

"I'm sorry, Grae." He rested a hand on her knee.

"No." The weight of his hand branded her skin through the fabric of her skirt and grounded her, in spite of the chaos churning in her chest. Before she could formulate what she knew she had to utter, her brain raced in a million and seven different directions. Snippets of images and scenes flashed across her frontal lobe. Her breath caught. In the time it took to fumble around in the dark for the window release button, panic took over, pulling her into its dark depths. *Where was the damn button?* She clawed at the door, gratitude spilling through her when the truck jolted to an abrupt stop. The handle landed beneath her fingers and she lurched from the cab. Night air entered her lungs but did little to ease the racing of her heart and the simmering in her gut.

Not again. Not another panic attack. Not now. She dropped to the ground, closed her eyes, and breathed. Each breath was a count. *One. Two. Three.* The grip on her lungs eased. *Four. Five. Six.* Her heartbeat slowed to almost normal. *Seven. Eight. Nine. Ten.* The knot in her stomach still yanked and tugged at her insides. She clutched her arms around herself and started the count over. Halfway through, the warmth of Charlie kneeling beside her made her lose count. *Damn him.* She turned to give him her best glare yet and was surprised when his hand slid over her back in soothing circles. His eyes never met hers. Instead, he stayed quiet, unobtrusive, but present. His even breathing and the play of his touch proved he was beside her, but his quiet demeanor was nothing like the Charlie Latham she thought she knew.

She watched him—silent, solid, statuesque—and realized her stomach had come untangled, her breathing had normalized, and the rapid flutter of her heart wasn't from panic. No, the flutter was all Charlie. *Damn.* Even in the worst of circumstances, he still had it.

"She's dead, isn't she?" The words felt wrong. She and her mom had a tumultuous history, no question about it, but her brain refused to accept the notion she'd never speak to her again. Never hear her singing off-tune in the kitchen to an oldies station on the radio. Never see her take the reins in a medical emergency, go head to head with whatever was on the other side of life, and win. She hadn't hugged her before she'd left the house this evening. When was the last time she'd even thought about hugging her? Had it really been so long that she couldn't remember?

"I'm sorry, Grae. I can take you somewhere else before I head over there."

Charlie's voice called her back to the present, where she could no longer pretend this was all a bad dream.

"No. Take me home. My father's responsible for this."

"How do you know that? Has he made a threat?" Charlie cocked his head and waited.

"Of course not, but his family hates us. Didn't you ever wonder what happened to him?"

"Not really. I just thought he was your mom's human fling." A crooked smile slipped across his face.

"You didn't just say that!" She landed a punch against his upper arm. A shiver overtook her.

Charlie brushed past her and opened the passenger door and waited while she debated how to climb in the cab without showing her rear. Sliding into her own sleek SUV wasn't a problem with a skirt and heels, but climbing up into the truck cab might prove difficult. After a last moment of hesitation, she squared her shoulders, gripped the handle inside the door, and hoisted herself in with as much dignity as she could muster. Miraculously, she landed in the seat without incident

Charlie's truck cut through the night, heading for the familiar twists and turns of Brass Castle Road, and Gracelynn's mind started making lists. She needed to find a way to clear out her place in Charlotte and find someone to handle her mom's estate here. She needed a place she could disappear, but still fend for herself. She pressed her fingers to her temples. A migraine brewed beneath the surface. Her world had shrunk tonight. There was no denying it. With Mom gone, she was exposed. Had she known her life would be lived on the run, she would've made different decisions. A job that allowed her to travel for one. Hell, maybe she would've even taken up running.

Her mom had always warned her a day like this could come. The man who contributed to her DNA would stop at nothing to find her, her mom always warned, but Gracelynn believed it a typical over-reaction from an overprotective parent. Now, she thought twice.

Reality snapped her out of her ridiculous reverie, and the truth stared her in the face. The father she never knew wanted her dead. Her mom had protected her with magic, until the one thing neither of them ever thought would happen, did. After waiting and wanting her whole life to show any signs of belonging to the community, when she least expected it, a double whammy hit her. First, the damn mind-reading. And then, the dreams. The ones where a certain six foot four, blond-haired man promised to love her forever.

Sadly, no one could love her now. It wasn't safe. *She wasn't safe.*

The lull in their conversation went unnoticed until Charlie broke the heavy silence. "I can protect you, you know."

His comment, as if he'd known what she'd been thinking, startled her. *Impossible.* Her mom had said telepathy was extremely rare among Elementals, and oftentimes wouldn't be seen for generations in a community.

Gracelynn sucked in a mouthful of air and settled her nerves. "No one can protect me. From everything Mom told me, my dad's family were Elemental hunters or something. Once he realized what Mom was, he went berserk. But a local witch coven owed her a favor, and as long as I didn't exhibit Elemental gifts, we were safe."

"So what's changed? I thought you never..."

"Peaked? Developed?" she suggested and raised a brow as she studied his profile while he drove.

"Oh you developed, all right."

The upturn of his lips sent butterflies to her gut and images of them in the bed of his truck raced to the front of her mind. She turned away, hoping he wouldn't see the heat creeping across her face. What the hell was she doing thinking about sex at a time like this? She slumped in the seat.

From the corner of her eye, the headlight beams struck pink. The Victorian house-shaped mailbox perched at the end of the drive and plucked at her heart. She and her mom had chosen the hot pink color for the mailbox. It had been a statement in her rebellious teenage phase when all the pure-bred Elemental kids were coming to grips with their gifts. They got super powers on their thirteenth birthday, but she got a neon pink mailbox. Take that. She was cool too. Of course, now it seemed ridiculous—trite even—but at the time, it had seemed like a good idea.

Charlie pulled down the long drive and parked in the small gravel lot her mom had added for her patients. It looked like every light in the house was on, and a strobe of red and blue shattered the night, thanks to the cruisers parked on the grass. What the hell was wrong with those assholes? Could they really not see the driveway or the damned parking lot? Selling the house would be a bitch if they rutted out the yard. The thought flickered through her mind in one instant, and in the next she wondered if she could take the mailbox. She'd never be able to use it, but it would act as a reminder of where she came from and who she was.

"Wait here. I'll go talk to the detective in charge." Charlie hopped out of the truck.

WIND'S SOLACE

Like hell would she sit and wait. She needed to know what happened. Besides, she'd gotten a mental flash from the killer back at The Outpost. Evil thoughts strong enough to break through the barrier of Eddie's drink gave her a leg up on all the officers inside her mother's house. If Charlie only knew, she'd be the biggest asset his police force had ever seen. How many *normal* people heard the thoughts in other people's heads? Not many, from what her mom claimed. Gracelynn was something of an enigma, considering her half-breed status.

Her gaze followed Charlie as he walked right up to the front door and let himself in. Once he disappeared from view, a lump formed in her throat. The darkness of the night weighed on her. Ominous. Heavy. Threatening. If the killer saw her leave the bar with Charlie, maybe he'd followed them. Her heart stuttered and her lungs froze. She refused to die sitting alone in Charlie's truck.

The smooth metal of the door-handle fit perfectly in her trembling hand, but before she shoved it open, she relaxed her mind and scanned the thoughts close enough to tap at her brain. None seemed malicious, but it didn't stop her from leaping from the truck and running. Her spiked heels sank in the ground with every footfall until her ankle screamed in pain. Without further consideration for her injury, she kicked off both shoes and continued her sprint across the cold grass.

Out of breath, she burst through the front door, scanning the foyer for any trace of Charlie.

"Ma'am? Can I help you?" asked an officer in full uniform.

Gracelynn shook her head and attempted to walk past him into the living room.

"I'm sorry. This is a crime scene. You can't go in."

"But..." she began, then changed her mind. Even with her gift, she struggled to differentiate the good guys from the bad guys at times. Case in point, Charlie. He seemed like a good one, but she knew better. The permanent scar in her heart proved she could be very wrong.

She took a deep breath, steadied her still shaking hands, and allowed the officers thoughts to infiltrate her overwhelmed mind. *Damn.* Heat whispered across her cheeks as the image of her tethered to a bed slithered through. The officer standing before her hovered over her as she tugged against the restraints. His penchant for using his cuffs while off duty steamrolled any other thought he might be having as he looked her up and down. *Ugh.* Was she surrounded by bad guys? Shaking her head, she stepped away from the officer, careful not to garner further attention.

She slipped back through the door into the night. The slate pavers leading from the front door to the office entrance, and around the back of the house, chilled her. She considered looking for her discarded heels, but decided against it as the brush of a thought touched her mind.

Gotta get them all. Mission isn't complete until they are all dead.

She raced along the path and ducked behind the house, and a sigh of relief escaped when she found the walkway to the back door unguarded. She took the wooden steps two at a time and peeked through the glass pane of the back door. Instant regret slammed deep in the pit of her stomach.

WIND'S SOLACE

In the threshold between the kitchen and the healing center, her mother lay with her eyes open and unseeing, mouth gaped in a frozen scream, and her head in a pool of darkening liquid that instinct named blood. Her mom hadn't gone quietly.

Reality was a bitch. She should've stayed home. Instead, excuses were made, and now her mom was dead. Unable to tear her eyes away from the gruesome scene in the kitchen she'd learned to cook in, a strangled sob stuck in her throat.

A familiar set of blue eyes appeared in her line of sight, blocking the view of her lifeless mom. Charlie motioned with his hand for her to back away from the door, before he stood and joined her in the backyard.

"I should've been here," she cried as soon as he closed the back door behind him, and tears trickled down her face.

"So you could wind up there on the floor beside her?" His harsh words didn't match the concerned look on his face.

"He must've found her," she tossed over her shoulder as she turned from the door. "I need to pack my stuff."

"Pack? Why? I can't imagine Sophie listing someone else as her beneficiary." Charlie slid a hand on her shoulder and squeezed.

"I'm dead if I stay." Her proclamation hung in the air as the truth robbed her of breath.

"Says who? You're more likely to end up dead next if you do run." He tightened his hold on her.

"My mom is laying in a pool of her own blood, and you're being a glib asshole," she yelled. She swung out of his grip and marched away from him.

"Let me in to get some stuff because, as you so eloquently put it, I don't want to be next."

"I can't let you remove anything from the house right now."

Her spine stiffened. "Why the hell not? It's my stuff." She didn't add the fact that somewhere in the darkness lurked the killer. She hadn't heard his thoughts since coming to the back of the house, but it didn't mean he was gone.

"It's a crime scene. We have to go through and determine what is evidence and what isn't."

"So you're telling me my underwear might be evidence?" She relished the stir of discomfort on his face.

"If it's covered in blood it is," he answered, matter-of-factly although the scrub of his hand across his chin said otherwise.

"I didn't kill her," she seethed. For heaven's sake, was there something wrong with his brain? Common sense didn't come with his good looks? Ugh. "Look at me. Do I look like a killer?"

"Grae…" His pitch dropped and the single syllable nickname stretched.

"Oh no, don't you dare. You know I wouldn't kill my mom."

"But the two of you aren't known for getting along."

"Do you really think I could've killed my mother? Of course we didn't get along—she kept me from knowing my dad, she forced me to grow up in a place where I never had a chance of fitting in, and when I needed her most, she found something else to be a bigger and more important priority. But that isn't reason enough to murder my own mother." Her hands flew through the air as her agitation grew.

She loved her mom. It wasn't always easy to love her, but she did, and losing her now was going to make getting rid of her *gift* damn near impossible. She stopped moving and turned her attention to the back door, where a uniformed officer stood watching them.

"Latham, can I talk to you for a minute?" The officer flitted a wary glance over Gracelynn. She felt the weight of his gaze when it landed at her bare feet. Yeah, this definitely wasn't the best first impression to give off to the men investigating her mom's death.

"Stay here," Charlie instructed with a wag of his finger, like maybe this time she'd listen to his command.

"Whatever," she huffed before shuffling down the wooden steps to stand in the cold grass.

She hadn't paid much attention to Charlie's attire at the bar—she'd been too busy sending him mental death rays—but now, she couldn't keep from noticing the way his jeans hung on his hips. Great ass, no use denying it. She jerked her gaze from his backside when he spun around and gave her a quizzical look.

She turned her back to the men, closed her eyes, and concentrated on their voices until she could distinguish their individual thought patterns. Charlie's thoughts were stunted little clips of only a couple of seconds or less—mere flashes. The other man, however, read like the ticker that runs along the bottom of a news program, broadcasting every single thing his mind held. The loudest and most recurring of his brilliant thoughts had to do with her. Between his fixation with the sway of her hips as she rocked from foot to foot trying to get warm, and her outburst exclaiming all the reasons she had to kill her mom, all he could imagine was a scenario with her behind the bullet-proof glass of his cruiser.

Uh-oh.

6

Random Thought # 1567 - For goodness sake, learn to take a hint when it comes your way.

❧

Charlie ground his molars together to keep from doing something stupid. Officer McNally was insistent that Grae should be taken down to the station and questioned, but the read Charlie got from him wasn't all on the level.

Shaking his head, he raised his voice and gave in to the man before him. "Look, I'll handle it, but not tonight." He nodded his head in Grae's direction. "She's been through too much already."

"So you're gonna let her go free? We both know family's the first suspect. The lady's student in there"—he yanked a notebook from his pocket and flipped through the pages—"Elma something...said herself the vic and her daughter weren't close. Yet, here she is, back in town, and now the nice lady's dead."

"I'll make sure she shows up at the station tomorrow," Charlie promised.

"Yeah? How?" McNally countered, rising to the balls of his feet.

For fuck's sake, this guy was annoying. Charlie tried to remember working with him in the past, but couldn't place him. He must be one of the newer recruits. He shrugged, "I'll bring her in myself. Okay?" The play of emotions that rolled over McNally's face matched the thoughts of doubt in the guy's mind.

This wasn't looking good for Grae. And if she wasn't upset enough, it was about to get a whole lot worse. Charlie kicked the toe of his boot in the dirt and cursed under his breath. She was gonna be pissed.

"Hey," Grae touched his shoulder. "Did you work it out that I can get inside and pack my things?"

Shit. Couldn't the woman take a hint? He'd said he'd take care of the situation, meaning keeping her out of the damn slammer; but no, that wasn't enough for her. He turned to McNally and waved his hand. "Officer McNally,"—he gestured from the officer, then toward her— "Gracelynn George, the deceased's daughter."

"Sorry for your loss," McNally muttered while he stared hard at the ground at Grae's feet.

A thought of deep red painted toes went through Charlie's mind. *Lovely.* It all made sense now. McNally had a thing for feet, and Grae's were as perfect as the rest of her. *Damn.* Now he was staring at her feet too. What the hell was wrong with him?

"Thanks. But can I get in there to pack my bags?"

"Grae..."

"Ma'am, the only place you're going is to an interrogation room," McNally jumped in, cutting him off.

"What are you talking about? I didn't kill my mother. Are you really going to waste time interrogating me when the real killer is out there? You guys are ridiculous." She glared at them both.

McNally's mouth dropped, and Charlie shook his head. With an attitude like that, he was going to have one hell of a time defending her innocence, an innocence he truly believed. Even without the added benefit of hearing her thoughts clearly, he wholeheartedly trusted she wasn't a killer. Someone who'd spent her teenage years reading to the sick and elderly, and feeding every stray within a five-town radius, wasn't destined to become a killer. Especially one so brutal as the one they were dealing with.

Despite her beef with the community, he didn't think for a second Grae would hurt someone intentionally. She was the 'love-them-and-leave them' type. He was Exhibit A in that defense. A wave of nostalgia rolled over him as the temptation to touch the woman he took countermeasures to forget grew into something hard to deny.

Her natural beauty wasn't only worn on her skin. She was beautiful deep down into her soul, and touching her stood the chance of diminishing that. He'd ruined her throughout their childhood. Now, he refused to cause her any more pain. The community had failed her. He'd failed her. And if he didn't think of something fast, the law would fail her too.

When the idea struck, it did so with the force of a pissed off bull. She'd hate him for what he was about to suggest. With a deep breath locked and loaded, he laid a reassuring hand on her shoulder. "We'll go to the station in the morning. Then, you can give your statement. Tonight, we've got to get you somewhere safe so you can rest."

"But my stuff," she pleaded.

"Your stuff will have to wait until they release the crime scene. In the meantime, we can scrounge up the basics." He steered her away from the house and toward the front lot where his truck waited.

"But I don't even have my purse, just my clutch with very little in it." She twisted back toward the house, ducking under his arm.

"You have enough for now. I'll see if I can get one of the detectives to bring it in tomorrow morning. 'Kay?" Charlie reassured her as he slipped his arm around her shoulder, anchoring her to his side so she couldn't wiggle away again.

McNally cleared his throat behind them. "Be there by nine sharp. I'd hate for the captain to put out a warrant for the both of you."

"Ten-four," Charlie called back and continued the forward momentum as he made a mental note to have a stern talk with the officer later. He bent his head close to hers and dropped his voice to a low growl. "Can't you take a hint? I'm sticking my neck out here for you, and all you keep doing is begging to get inside the murder scene. What are you thinking?"

"I'm thinking about saving my own ass. Because I'm pretty sure I'll be on the slab next to Mom in the morgue before you can clear my name. I'd bet anything my dad is behind this," she repeated.

Her bare feet stumbled over the gravel of the parking area and he released her from his iron grip until she reached the grass. Her head dipped low and her ass rose into the air as she appeared to be searching for something. He stepped closer only to see the satisfied look on her face when she rose with her pair of fuck-me shoes in her hands.

She shimmied into the shoes until she noticed his gaze fully on her. He should look away. He knew he should. But—*Damn!*—He really had no interest in looking anywhere else. The moonlight played on her dark hair, while her toned legs and tight ass screamed *"Look at me!"* thanks to the heels.

Charlie swallowed back the apology his mother would want him to utter, because once he started apologizing to this girl, he was afraid he'd never stop.

Killing her tomorrow isn't soon enough.

A different voice from the one he'd heard at the bar seeped through his mind. A quick glance around the yard confirmed they were still alone, despite the threat. He needed Grae near. Now.

Before he could take a step, she was folding herself into his side, her face paler than before. Perhaps she could sense the evil nearby. He pulled her close and whispered in her ear.

"I won't let anything happen to you," he promised. "Follow me."

He guided them over the grass to his truck and opened the passenger door. Without waiting for her to boost herself in, he reached into the glovebox and pulled out his .38. After a quick scan for thoughts closing in on them, he swung his back on the truck and steadied his trigger hand. When nothing registered in his mind after a minute, he turned to Grae. Fear etched across her beautiful face and pulled at his heartstrings.

"Do you trust me?" The cliché of his question occurred to him only after it left his mouth. If he could've pulled it back and tried again, he would've, but she answered before he could reword his question.

"Yes."

A single word had never meant so much to him. The weight of his responsibility crashed down on him as he closed her door and rounded the front of his truck. He tucked the handgun into his waistband and slid into the driver's seat. He needed to take her someplace safe. A hotel wouldn't do. Nor would a B&B, even though he happened to know one whose owner was more *other* than human.

The most logical answer stared him in the face. As much as he wanted to believe someone else could protect Grae better than himself, he'd never take the risk. Not with her. Never. If she was out of sight, he'd likely spend his night in the truck parked in front of wherever she slept anyway. It only made sense to have her under the very same roof he was under.

With two dead bodies fitting a description similar to hers, and now her mother added to the mix, he couldn't shake the feeling that maybe she was right. Maybe her father *had* found her and was as awful as she suggested he might be. Despite their history being anything but pretty, he couldn't in good conscience send Grae away and not know if she was safe.

He steered the truck back out to the main thoroughfare that ran through Harmony and kept a careful eye on the rearview to ensure they weren't being followed. At a stop sign several blocks away from her mom's house, he exhaled all the pent-up breath he'd been unable to release since leaving Grae's home. There wasn't another vehicle in sight, and nothing but deserted road stretched before them.

He glanced at his friend and caught her swiping at her eyes. She was gonna be mad when he told her, he was certain of it, but why exactly she would be upset would probably be a bit of a mystery. Unlike most people, her thoughts didn't just worm into his brain and tumble around. He had to actively search them out, and even then, they still came through like static on an old transistor radio. It had occurred to him that her thoughts weren't as accessible as most while they'd been standing in the backyard with McNally, back when she'd tried to get inside the house. The look on her face had been one that said piss and vinegar ran through her veins, but her thoughts were eerily quiet.

Thinking back to when they were teenagers, he hadn't been as practiced at filtering out people's thoughts as he now was, part of Grae's appeal had been his inability to read her mind. During their childhood, he'd enjoyed not knowing her every musing. Instead, every time she opened her mouth, it was a surprise, —no matter whether she joked, or better yet, put her lips on his. There had been an overwhelming sense of connection between them that he hadn't felt with women he could *hear*. To this day, he missed the particular type of quiet Grae offered.

He navigated the truck down Brass Castle, swung a wide right onto route 519, and a quick left onto the road leading him home. They sped by the old Presbyterian Church and its cemetery, took another hard left, and raced the sound of owls as they pushed ever closer to River Road. With every passing minute, his breath evened and his white-knuckle grip on the steering wheel loosened.

In places where the road was only bordered by train tracks laid beside the river's edge, a sense of calm descended in the truck. When a sigh escaped from his passenger's lips, he remembered just how much she had loved coming down here as a kid. They'd spent lots of time at his grandmother's house in the summers, swimming and flying over the water on a tire swing.

His grandmother used to tell him Grae continued her summer tradition after he'd gone off to college. He'd come home one weekend, early into his sophomore year, and found her swinging from the old tire swing. The fire engine-red bikini had branded itself into his brain for years. If he closed his eyes, he was sure he could call up the image in all its technicolor glory without any problem.

He shook the thought from his mind and flicked the high beams to navigate a one-lane stretch of the road. Soon, the landscape changed and the road veered from the river. Curves wound them around until his driveway appeared at the edge of his vision. He slowed the truck and pulled in, making a quick U-turn, before he parked and gave thanks that Maureen had left his home standing.

"Where are we?" Her voice sounded heavy.

Whether from grief or fatigue, he wasn't sure, but it didn't stop the worry from creeping into his chest. "Someplace safe." He cut the engine and sat in the dark silence waiting for something, anything, to come from the woman beside him.

"*Your* someplace safe?"

She didn't miss a thing. He shifted in his seat and withdrew his firearm from his waistband. "Yeah. I needed to convince McNally you'd definitely show up at the precinct tomorrow. Besides, with the dead bodies turning up, I didn't think a hotel was a good option." He'd exaggerated the part about McNally, but the rest was true.

"How many bodies?"

He paused in his attempt to lock his precinct-issued gun in the glove compartment, shocked. "What?"

"You said 'the dead bodies.' How many are there?"

He could feel her stare in the darkness, heavier than a prizefighter sitting on his chest. He sat back in his seat, debating how to respond.

"There are always dead people, Grae," he answered, hoping it would be enough to end her line of questioning.

"But they aren't all females that look like Mom and me, are they?"

Her pointed question sent a chill down his spine. "Who said they look like you?" He ran through every word he'd uttered in her presence and tried to pinpoint a single time he'd mentioned the other dead women. He couldn't come up with it.

Shit. Maybe McNally was right, and she had something to do with Sophie's death after all. Maybe the person feeling guilt in the bar was her. She'd looked pretty bad. Perhaps it'd been the guilt over what she'd done. And here he was bringing her to his home. *Damnit.* He needed more sleep so he'd stop making rookie mistakes.

"Never mind. I thought I saw something in the paper." She shifted in the seat and fumbled for the door handle. "Mind if I walk to the end of your property? If I'm not mistaken, the Delaware must run behind here."

"It does. Just be careful. The edge is a bit of a drop off," he cautioned, following her from the cab. As they moved around the rear of the truck and reached the end of the driveway, a floodlight blinked on from the rear corner of the house.

She slipped off her heels mid-step once they hit the grass, and the movement as fluid and graceful as the memory of her arched body flying through the air on the tire swing. He followed her between the few trees that separated the grassy area of the backyard from the dirt and rocky shoreline leading to the river.

He stopped a few feet away, but watched with a careful eye as she walked right up to the edge. Even in the darkness, she looked stunning. Hell, maybe it was because of the moonlight on her pale skin that he couldn't tear his eyes away. Or maybe it was the way she visibly relaxed the moment she dipped her toes into the cold water.

She splashed her bare foot in the water a few more times like he imagined a mermaid missing home might. "Just because I'm not fighting you about staying here, doesn't mean I'm going to sleep with you," she called, her words shattering the silence.

"I never said anything about sleeping together," he replied, offended.

"Oh, I know. But you were always a bit of a playboy, and I have no interest in rekindling anything with you for a night." She looked at him over one shoulder, her eyes wide and bright in the moonlight.

"Rekindle? We got close for a few months when we were teenagers. That's hardly anything to re-kindle," he countered, grateful she didn't have any way of knowing just how hard he was from hearing her mention the idea of them sleeping together. He studied her slumped shoulders and bowed head. *Definitely not the posture of a killer*, he reasoned. She looked downright fragile. From their past, he knew she was anything *but* the glass slipper-kind of woman. No. His Grae was more the golden arm bands of strength-kind of woman. Which, if he really thought about it, meant her behavior at the crime scene had likely been more a self-preservation method, than a true lack of sorrow.

Her panic attack at the side of the road earlier was the only evidence of her having a single weakness. Possibly even the only sign in all his years of knowing her.

He'd seen the effect grief had on people, one too many times, if anyone wanted the truth. But seeing it on her, the strongest person he knew, had almost been his undoing. She'd suffered so much in her life. Never knowing her father, never quite fitting in, never really connecting. If he could do anything to change her future, he would. But first, he had to ensure her safety. He reached into his pocket and slid his phone into his palm. "I'll be right back, I need to make a call."

He walked far enough away that she couldn't overhear him, but was still able to see her, then scrolled through his contacts and selected the one person with the skills to protect her life aside from himself. The ringer droned on and on and on until a gruff "Hello?" came over the line.

"Hey, buddy. I hate to do this, but can I ask you a favor?"

"What?" Sleep lined Colin's voice.

"I need you to come out here and run patrol for me. You mind?"

"Run, *run*?" His friend knew him too well. Although it wasn't often Charlie asked others for help, he'd stepped in enough times for others to have earned the occasional goodwill call to action favor.

"If you wouldn't mind."

"Okay, but why?" Colin's voice deepened as it cleared.

"Would it offend you if I said I can't tell you why?" Charlie asked, his tone hushed so the woman in question wouldn't overhear.

"Not in the least. What am I looking for?"

"Anyone who doesn't belong on the property." The answer flew out of his mouth. "There should only be you, me, and a woman. No one else."

"Understood. I'll be there in ten. Listen for the howl."

"Will do, my friend. Thanks. Oh! Before you come, can you call Simon and make sure Elms is okay? Something happened at Sophie's, and in her current condition, I want to make sure someone's there looking out for her." After Colin agreed, Charlie clicked off the phone and joined Grae at the water's edge. The scent of vanilla and flowers danced on the slight breeze. He closed his eyes and breathed it in, letting it wash over his senses and toy with his mind. Because somewhere, deep on the very edge of his conscious awareness, he knew the smell. Cherished it, even. It remained imprinted on his brain. Linked him to her. Made her something he could never have. *His.*

With a quick tug at his waistband, he adjusted the evidence of his derailed train of thought, and prayed to all that was holy she hadn't noticed.

7

Random Thought # 596 - Revenge sex is like eating revenge brownies; you leave feeling satisfied and disappointed all at the same time.

Gracelynn smiled to herself. Flashes of random thoughts blinked across her mind as fast as Charlie's pulse beat. She wondered if he knew how much he projected. A blip of discomfort flared in his groin. She'd like to have been able to say she was a lady about it and didn't glance at his zipper, but anyone who knew her would call *bullshit* in a New York nanosecond.

WIND'S SOLACE

The darkness of the night didn't reveal what she knew would be there, but her imagination filled in the image just fine. She turned back to the river, sat in the grass, and exhaled a deep breath. This was heaven on Earth. The sound of the river lapping at the shore mingled with all the nighttime sounds of fall in the sticks, and merged into a soundtrack of peace and resentment.

The peace she struggled to accept after the night she'd endured here—in Harmony, against all odds—now more alone than ever. She'd lived among the Elementals as a human. Yet, among the humans, she existed as something not quite the same, despite her lack of gifts. It wasn't that people even realized there was anything different about most of the town's inhabitants, but she knew. And in this case, knowledge didn't give her an ounce of power. Nope. Instead, it gave her a sense of overwhelming inferiority. Inferior to the supernaturals, and yet still inferior to everyone else who could live a blissfully ignorant life.

The air warmed as Charlie plopped down next to her. She watched as he shucked his work boots and socks and dipped his feet in beside hers. A second later, he pulled them from the frigid waters with a curse on his lips.

"Not as warm as in the summer," she teased.

"How can you stand it? It's freezing." He rubbed his feet and met her eyes.

"I think I'm just numb." It was the truest statement she'd made all night. Her heart sank. A long time ago, they'd been friends—the kind of friendship people never expected to lose when life gets in the way. Hell, they'd even stayed friends after the cluster fuck that was her thirteenth birthday and the dating faux pas. Yet the idea of trusting him with anything important to her sat just outside her grasp.

"Well, you've had your feet in there a while," he agreed breaking her from the dialogue in her head.

"Not my feet, silly. Me. Mom was brutally murdered, I'm wanted for questioning, and I'm almost positive I'll be your next dead body. With all that swimming around in my head, I think my body is just numb—like a protective coating, since my mind is such a mess right now." She gave her feet a gentle kick to demonstrate her point. The cold barely registered.

"I believe you didn't kill Sophie. Does that help?"

She met his steady gaze and was surprised to see the earnestness behind his words etched in the lines of his face.

"Believe it or not, it does." A howl sliced through the night. "I forgot there's wildlife around here." She laughed as a shiver overtook her body.

"No wildlife where you live now?"

"Do Palmetto bugs count?"

"What the heck are Palmetto bugs? They sound like a disease or something." He slid his socks on and stuffed his feet into his boots without lacing them.

"They're kind of like roaches but terrifying in their own right."

Out of the trees trotted a large brown dog. "Holy shit! What's that?" She scrambled to her feet and jumped behind Charlie's back, putting him between herself and the animal.

The dog stopped in its tracks and gave a growl.

"Don't be scared, he's a regular." Charlie reached out a hand.

She watched the dog sniff the air before taking a careful step in their direction. "Is he dangerous? I don't see a collar."

"He's a stray who comes around for dinner some nights. Why don't we go inside, and I'll make a little something for us all?" Charlie nodded toward the animal and got to his feet.

Faster than lightening, a vision of hamburgers went through her head, but not in the same pattern she attributed to Charlie. Could she read the dog's thoughts?

No. That was crazy. Dogs didn't have human thoughts. She gave the animal a curious look and it trotted into the darkness, leaving nothing but the sound of brush crunching under its paws in its wake.

"Does it have a name?" she asked as she caught up to Charlie in the trees that sheltered the water from the view of the street.

"Does what have a name?" Confusion laced his words.

"The dog. Does it have a name?" she insisted, "A dog that comes around often deserves one, even if it's only a stray." She stopped long enough to slip her heels back on, but cursed the love of gravel in Harmony when she lost her footing in the driveway.

"Gotcha," Charlie whispered, wrapping his arms around her to keep her from meeting the ground with her knees.

She slid her hands along his biceps to support herself and enjoyed feeling small in his strong grasp. At over six feet in heels, it was nice to feel dainty in a man's hold.

Her pulse stepped up its pace when a whiff of sandalwood tickled her nose, and the press of her body against his solid form registered in her brain. Holy smokes, Charlie Latham had indeed grown up nicely.

For the first time since setting eyes on him in the bar, she reconsidered her stance on all things Charlie. He was everything all her past disasters of relationships weren't—strong, independent, wild. It was a sexy combination on any man she supposed, but add those baby blue eyes of his, and it was downright irresistible.

Even if it meant losing her heart to him again? She considered the possibility and relished the knowledge she'd grown up a bit as well since their last time together. She could read his mind for goodness sake, which meant she'd be able to know what he was thinking at any given moment.

Like right now, she knew he was working really hard to keep her from pressing against his thigh, because he was aiming to keep his erection a secret.

A smile tugged at her cheeks and she did what any shameless Jersey Girl would do when tangled up with a hunky man—she leaned the hell in. His breath caught in his throat and she moved in for the kill—balls to the wall—or at least breasts to his chest. Her body plastered to his, she held fast to him and brushed her lips over his. Unlike his kiss in the bar, this was soft, sensual, simple. Need coursed through her body, humming like an electric current, and Charlie stiffened beneath her intrusion.

His thoughts raced through his mind and dripped into hers like paint splattering on a canvas; confusion mixed with desire, dipped in a healthy dose of lust. Instinct took over and she deepened the kiss. Her tongue played along the seam of his lips, daring him to open to her demands.

A beat of time passed, and she knew he'd give in before his hands clung to her and his lips parted, possession and passion on his mind. This kiss took her to a new level of awareness. Not only could she hear the thoughts racing through his mind, but she could feel the emotions welling inside his chest.

Her empty declaration from earlier not to sleep with him faltered, as her mind begged her body to reconsider. Flashes of desire punctuated the pleas, promising her this would be a one-time thing. A way to de-stress, escape her grief, and pass the time until she could escape this town and the person hunting her. She was certain one night with Charlie would cure what ailed her.

"Grae..."

Her name, a mere moan on his lips, drove her faster toward the distraction his body offered. She ran her fingers over the hard planes of his chest and whimpered in the back of her throat. If that didn't convince Charles Latham she wanted him, she wasn't sure what would.

8

Random Thought # 7,893 - Sometimes you gently pump the breaks to avoid a disaster. Other times, accelerate and steer into the skid while hoping for a miracle.

For the first time in a long time, the silence in Charlie's head annoyed him. Grae was doing her best to play tonsil hockey with him right there in his driveway, and all he wanted was to hear her thoughts tell him why. The honorable thing would be to back away from her hot body, walk her to his guest room, bid her goodnight, and take the coldest shower he could stand. Yeah. That would be the honorable thing to do.

Too bad his arms were pulling her closer and he was wrapping his hands in her long dark silken mane of hair. His thigh also had a mind of its own as it pressed against her core. His tongue, the last holdout before his brain gave up the struggle, mated with hers in his mouth before claiming the sweetness beyond her lips. Yeah. He wasn't cut out for honorable. He was more the *claim what was his*-kind of guy.

The temptation Grae's kiss offered tightened every nerve ending into a ball of white-hot heat. Urged forward by the combination of his lust and another moan vibrating through her, every reasonable thought left his head. All he could think about was wrapping her legs around his waist and sinking into her. He dropped his hands from her hair, then slid them down her back and over the curve of her ass. The material of her skirt was soft, maybe suede, and it bunched easily in his hands as he worked it up her legs until his fingers landed on warm, smooth skin. He slid his hands over the swells until each palm held a cheek of her ass.

A little shimmy of her hips, and he thought he would lose his mind as her heat seeped through the denim of his jeans. Tired of innocent kisses, he pulled his lips from hers and traced the outer shell of her ear with his tongue until she shimmied again, then whispered, "I want you. Now. Here."

Grae leaned back enough to meet his eyes when she nodded. "How about your truck?" A single eyebrow rose as a sly smile crossed her face.

All the blood in his head rushed south of his waistband. His clothes were too tight. Too bulky.

Too *much*. Everything in his head drifted to an earlier fantasy involving Grae, the moon, and the bed of the truck in question. *Damn*. There was no way he could pass this up.

"The bed." His words shook. He tipped his chin toward the vehicle so there was no misunderstanding. "Now."

She wiggled out of his grasp, offered a devious smile, and crooked a long finger in his direction.

"You'll have to help me. These heels aren't made for climbing into truck beds."

Fuck. She looked good standing there, barely covered by her skirt as the moonlight played with the shadows on her face.

"Keep the heels." He grabbed her around the waist and pulled her against him.

She felt right. Like she was made for him. The thought trickled through his mind, giving him pause. He was notoriously outspoken in his disagreement that the community was at the mercy of some higher being who dictated mates, but Grae constantly worked her way under his skin at every turn. He'd never be free from her appeal—he'd already spent years trying to deny it. She wiggled against him, sending every ounce of attention to the problem growing in his jeans. Ignoring it wouldn't make it go away, but maybe he could convince his brain to remember she was traumatized. She'd seen her mother dead only an hour ago, and was potentially the next victim. Too bad the only part of him thinking clearly resided in his pants.

A deep inhale did little to clear his mind. Instead, it slid her deeper into his senses, wrapped him in her warmth, and wagered with him to take a risk for once where Grae was concerned. Playing it safe with her had been the downfall of their relationship years ago, back when he'd fallen in love with her. There were just too many rules and too many stigmas about her age and the question of her Elemental status in regards to fated mating. He'd blown it then by leaving, but now, he couldn't risk her running out on him. Not when he'd sworn to protect her.

A sound rumbled behind him in the night, punctuating the small sliver of resolve he tried to grasp. Grace stilled in his arms.

"Is that the regular?"

"What?" Charlie's mind raced to catch the meaning of her words.

"The noise. Was it the stray?" A shiver coursed through her body as another low rumble sounded, closer this time than before.

Blood made its way back to Charlie's brain and he searched the night for his friend, Colin. The growling persisted, and from the darkness, a large cream-colored beast emerged slowly, its eyes on them. The hair on Charlie's arms stood on end as the realization it wasn't Colin hit home. There had been recent reports of a bobcat or something stalking local farms, but this was Charlie's first time seeing it. The animal's nose rose into the air, sniffing as it crouched lower.

"That's not my friend." Charlie moved slowly so as not to trigger the animal. He situated himself between the beast and Grae. He would never hear the end of it from his boss if the woman involved with an active case was eaten alive by a damn bobcat while in his custody. Instinct moved his hand to his waistband for his service revolver be-fore he remembered it was in the truck.

The animal let out what sounded like a scream as it stalked closer. A low growl from another an-imal cut through the night. The cat took its eyes off them as if it sensed the presence of the dog racing from the woods. Relief surged through Charlie's body as he watched Colin, in his choco-late lab form, tearing through the trees. Grae dug her fingers into the back of his shirt when Colin leapt like a well-aimed bullet at the cat. Snarls warred with screams as the two tumbled in the night.

"That's my guy." Charlie pointed toward the wresting duo, unable to keep the pride out of his tone. "Let's get you inside." He turned and tried to shuffle Grae toward the house, but she refused and pushed against his chest.

"Shouldn't we do something?" Her breath caught as the cat planted its jaws into Colin's flank. "He's going to need help." Her words were sure, unquestioning. "Where's your gun?"

Without thought, he gathered her into his arms and lifted her into the bed of the truck. "Stay put," he ordered as he opened the driver's side door and reached across the dash to the glovebox. He fumbled with his keys to unlock the compart-ment before his fingertips slid across the cold steel of his gun and withdrew it from the dark depths. By the time he rounded the truck, Colin was chas-ing the cat into the woods, and a crash of thunder broke the night as rain poured down.

Crisis averted, he turned to help Grae down and found her with her chin upturned to the sky as raindrops slid over her like a lover caressing her face. Rain streaked through her hair and clung to her skin, but the smile on her lips carried away any concern he might've had.

"You okay?" His voice seemed to startle her, as if she'd completely forgotten where she was and what had been going on.

"Yeah." She looked around as if seeing him for the first time. "I'm not sure what happened. I remember thinking how I wished something would scare the bobcat away. That's what it was, right? A bobcat?"

As she spoke, the rain slowed to a stop. A freak thunderstorm.

"I think so," he agreed and unlatched the tailgate. "Did you see where the dog went? Was he hurt?"

"I don't think he was hurt, but he did chase the cat off into the woods." She crawled to the edge of the tailgate and lowered herself so that her feet dangled above the ground and her shoulder leaned into his.

"I hope he's okay."

"I'm sure he's fine. A little pissed off the cat got a bite in on his ass, but okay."

Charlie stared open-mouthed. "What did you just say?"

"The dog. He's okay." A shrug added to her response.

Unable to let it go, Charlie opened his mind and allowed the full force of his gift to seek out the answers in her head. This wasn't something he did lightly, but Grae was keeping something from him. He could tell.

His gift reached into the night and found Colin's wavelength. Grae had been right. He wasn't hurt, so long as his pride wasn't part of the equation. But when it came to Grae's mind, there always seemed to be something guarding her thoughts, keeping them hidden from his usual means.

Content in the knowledge they were alone, He cocked his head to the side and considered his options. When he was a young telepath, Sophie George, Grae's mom had counseled him on how to close off his thoughts, and also how to break down walls of those he couldn't access. He'd been warned sex was a gateway to the most intimate sharing of those tucked away thoughts. Sophie'd cautioned him to make sure he never opened himself to his partners unless he was ready to potentially bond with them, because the experience could be so intense. He never imagined he'd consider doing it with her daughter, but the need to protect her far outweighed his ethical dilemma.

A quick hop and he was seated beside her. The entire left side of his body touched her right side. He tried again, but the limited contact wasn't enough. He slipped his hand to her bare knee and caressed her skin.

"Where were we before the interruption?" He raised a brow and wiggled it.

"I think you were telling me to leave my shoes on," she confessed and slid farther back into the bed, breaking the contact.

"Well, can you blame me? Heels like those deserve to be appreciated, right?"

"Damn right they do," she agreed. "These bad boys cost a fortune and should see action." Grae leaned back on her elbows, showcasing her ample chest in her rain-soaked blouse.

"Aren't you cold?"

"Nope. You?" She kicked a foot into the air and studied her shoe from her prone position.

"Uh-uh. But I think maybe we should get you out of those wet clothes. You know, make sure you don't catch a chill." He shrugged out of his flannel shirt and inclined his head her way.

"See, there's a little problem with that." She slid her fingers to the buttons holding her top together and paused. "If I take these off, I won't have anything to wear. If you'll recall, you refused to let me pack a bag." She popped the top button and waited.

Saliva pooled in his mouth as the top of her breast gleamed. It took every bit of gentlemanly restraint he possessed not to rip the top completely off.

"I have clothes you could wear," he offered. "Although, I think I'd like very much to see you without clothes." He slid farther into the bed of the truck and lay back, staring at the now-clear sky. It was the only way he could concentrate.

"I'm sure you would, but I have a confession to make."

He immediately rolled to his side and stared at her. If she was going to admit to killing Sophie, he needed to see her face when she uttered the words.

"Oh?"

"Remember earlier when I asked if my underwear could be evidence?"

"How could I forget?"

"Well, that's what I need to confess." She dropped her voice to a whisper, "I'm not wearing any underwear. I never do. What doesn't exist can't exactly convict me, can it?"

The smile that played across her face sent blood to pool in his groin. "You're killing me, you know that?"

"Then do something about it, Charlie. I offered you exactly what you wanted, so take it. Make me forget tonight happened. Please."

He watched as she slid her next two buttons open to reveal a satin and lace bra. She might be going commando beneath the skirt, but the contrast of the silky white material covering her breasts with her skin had his head back in lust-filled clouds.

Before she could undo another button, he grabbed her hands, raised them above her head, and pinned her to the bed with his body.

"I could've planned this for a thousand years and never imagined it possible." He removed one hand from hers and slid the back of his knuckles down her cheek until his thumb came to rest on her lips. Like a long-lost lover who knew his every wish, she parted her lips and flicked her tongue against the pad.

As soon as she sucked his finger into the wet depths of her mouth, he knew he only wanted to share this kind of sensual exchange of thoughts with her and opened his mind to hers again. This time he caught glimpses of things he never expected. Mirror images of his own desire reflected back at him. Fun house mirrors they had to be though, because every image was slightly distorted, as if she'd seen his thoughts and made her own decision about each and every one.

Grae struggled beneath him and nipped his thumb. "What the hell are you doing?"

Rising, he did something he hadn't done in many years. He shut down all thoughts in his head. "Grae," he warned. "Tell me why you're here."

"Tonight? Because someone killed my mom, and you won't let me leave." She scooted to a sitting position and buttoned her blouse.

"No. Here in Harmony. I thought you swore you'd never come back to a place controlled by the community." He moved to the end of the bed, intent on putting as much physical distance between them as he could. If his suspicions were correct, it would only help him.

"Mom asked me to come here." She worked her bottom lip between her teeth and refused to make eye contact. "She was going to help me learn how to control my gift."

"I thought you didn't develop a gift." He stuttered as bits of earlier conversation connected in his head. "That's why they're killing woman who look like you. You developed an Elemental gift." He immediately wished he could withdraw the accusing tone accompanying his words. Instead, he lowered his voice and softened his features. "Earlier, you mentioned a protection spell," he offered and waited for her to finish the thought.

After a solid minute, she nodded.

"Tell me," he demanded.

"Why? Who are you to ask me about something so private? I never asked you what your Fate-given gift was. In all our time as friends, I never once asked you to show me what made you so damn special. And now, in less than a couple of hours, you just demand that I share the most private thing in my life with you? Well, fuck you,

Charlie Latham. I don't owe you anything." She crossed her arms over her chest and refused to look at him.

"You know we can't share our gifts with humans. You obviously aren't human. You're Elemental, which means *now* we can talk about our gifts." He paused and reached a hand to her. "I'll make you a deal. Show me yours and I'll show you mine."

"What are we, twelve? Come on, Charlie. Don't be ridiculous."

"How about if I go first?" He released her hand and slid off the tailgate before turning toward her. "You didn't kill your mom," he started.

"No kidding. I've told you that multiple times." Annoyance coated her words as her fingers twined together in her lap.

"I know you have. But I know you didn't do it for a fact. Just like I know you heard the killer tonight. Once at the bar, and twice at your mom's house." He tapped a finger against the bed liner while he waited for her to speak. When she remained silent, he continued. "I know, because I could see it in your mind. Just as I suspect you saw this,"—he gestured to her in the back of his truck—"in mine."

With the spotlight adding to the moonlight, he witnessed something he'd never seen before...Grae crying. Quietly at first, then heaving sobs. She appeared so wounded and small it was hard for him to look at her. He believed this show of weakness was one she'd regret. Then, knowing her, she'd be pissed he let her carry on.

"Let's get inside. The last thing I need is to explain our primary suspect got eaten alive by a bobcat."

"Are you telling me you're also telepathic?" She swiped at the train of tears and scooted to the end of the tailgate.

"See for yourself." He meant it less as a challenge and more as a peace offering, but the set of her jaw said she read more into his simple phrase.

So you can hear me thinking I wish the bobcat hadn't interrupted us? Her teases slithered through his mind.

He smiled and gave her a wink before responding mentally. *Oh, I'm reading that loud and clear. I really wanted to see if you were going commando under that skirt.*

Her eyes widened and she shuddered.

"Look, Grae, I'm sure this is strange for you, but once you get used to it, it's not really that bad. And you can learn to control it," he offered when her disbelief wafted through his mind. It was downright refreshing to have someone understand what he'd been dealing with for so many years.

Have you been able to hear all my thoughts tonight?

No. You've been pretty guarded, he admitted. "But I think you've decided to open up to me, now you know you aren't alone." He placed one hand on hers and used his other to tip her chin up toward him. "Tell me you don't feel more comfortable."

"I do," she agreed with a timid nod.

"And what do you think of the thoughts running through my brain right now?" He leaned close enough to get a good whiff of the scent he knew only as Grae.

He let his mind run free, showcasing his favorite thoughts of her over the years. Ones he never shared with anyone. The red bikini one snaked out before he could attempt to pull it back.

A small gasp brought his attention to her lips.

"I remember that day. I wanted you to notice me so badly. I wanted you to see what you'd left behind. To see I could compete with all the college girls you were dating. To see I could be enough." Her voice trembled and she clenched his hand tight.

"Oh, I noticed you, all right." He lowered his lips and brushed a tender kiss on her cheek. "And I noticed every other guy there noticing you. It nearly killed me." He stroked up her chin. "I even had to threaten Robbie."

"The Wind with the man-bun, back before it was a thing? The one who played college football?"

"Yup. He planned to ask you out. Said he thought you'd go down faster than a quarterback whose defense left him wide open."

"No!"

"I don't know if that was exactly it, but he alluded to doing something a girl your age shouldn't have been subjected to."

"I wasn't much younger than you," she chided. "I was old enough to make my own decisions, you know. I could've told him 'no.'"

"Sure, you could've, but I was worried you wouldn't." The truth was hard to admit, but knowing she'd be able to pluck it straight from his brain made it a necessary evil.

"Oh? Were you jealous?"

Her teasing tone did little to lighten the lead balloon he felt in his gut when thinking of her with another guy. Then he remembered. She was engaged. She already belonged to someone else. And here he was, trying to convince himself it was okay to act on his long-held feelings.

I'm not really engaged.

The thought exploded in his head.

I was mad and wanted you to eat your heart out. "Sorry."

Relief flooded his system as her verbal apology hung in the air between them. He wanted to scold her. Tell her he didn't appreciate her games. Make her feel bad. But deep down, he knew he wouldn't do any of those things. Instead, he'd start over and try to convince her he'd changed. Show her his worth. They could be something more than they once only wished to be.

"Stop right there. All those thoughts are too much to track," she moaned, rubbing her temples. "I can't keep up with you when you're thinking so many things so quickly."

Charlie concentrated on shutting the mental door to his thoughts. He needed to remember his personal thoughts belonged tucked away. Safe. The iron gate in his mind crashed securely into place.

9

Random Thought # 79 - Being vulnerable is like being stood up by your own courage- painful and embarrassing.

Shit! Whatever Charlie had done to quiet his mind hurt like a damn frying pan to the head. Gracelynn wondered if it was possible to have brain trauma from his mental shove.

"What the hell was that for?" She rubbed at her temples and refused to meet his eye. What did she expect? Opening up to Charles Latham had a long history of causing her some sort of pain.

"Sorry. I'm not accustomed to having someone able to hear all my thoughts."

"It's fine." She eyed him up and down before continuing. "I imagine it takes some getting used to," she agreed as she hopped off the tailgate. Her heels teetered on the gravel as they begged for purchase. Charlie's hand shot out to offer support, but she batted it away. Already, her vulnerability echoed with regret in her heart. Forgetting his ability to hurt her with such ease was her mistake. One she refused to make a second time. She stalked around the truck to retrieve her small clutch from the passenger floorboard.

"Grae."

Warning rang clear in his tone, but she ignored him and the newly-outstretched arm he'd offered as she slammed the door.

"Look, Charlie, you wanted me here. I'm here. You said I had to stay until morning. I'm staying until morning. I'm a suspect in your murder investigation, making anything between us... difficult." She teetered toward the house and out of his orbit, willing the distance between them to give her the strength she needed to sell the point she was about to make. "A long time has passed. I've moved on. You've moved on. There's no reason to dabble in the what-ifs."

His jaw dropped. Charlie stood perfectly still as disbelief played across his features and a sense of satisfaction soothed her soul. Being separated, thinking became easier, less crowded. Hell, she could even breathe easier. Miracle of miracles. *Distance* from Charles Latham could cure all that ailed her. Now, she needed to maintain it.

Before she could ask where she'd be sleeping, he brushed past her and headed toward the front of the stilted ranch home. As he walked, he whistled, shattering the silence and stillness of the night. The chocolate lab raced from the tree line and fell into step beside

Charlie, more an equal than a timid stray looking for handouts. She didn't have much time to consider it before she lost sight of them as they rounded the corner of the house.

Alone again.

Her knack for finding any situation where she could be an outsider was in full force. Gracelynn teetered, still unbalanced, across the drive, despite only the small clutch now hanging across her body weighing her down. Maybe guilt and life lessons, combined with rain-soaked clothes, weighed more than she gave them credit for.

When her feet landed on the cement sidewalk, she let out a breath. Tonight she'd sleep here, and tomorrow she'd answer all the questions she could regarding her mother's death. She'd do whatever it took to convince them she was innocent. Then, by tomorrow night, she'd be in the wind. Off to a new place, ready for a new start. One that would be as temporary as this one perhaps, but she'd figure it out. Like all mortals gifted in one way or another, she'd trained her entire life to live a transient existence. Why should coming back to Harmony change that?

She took Charlie's steps one at a time, her feet slowed by sudden truth. This might be her last time here. Her last hurrah in a place she'd once thought of as home. And worse, all because Fate fucked with her life and gave with one hand, while taking away with the other, she was homeless.

10

Random Thought # 923 - "Now or Never" meets
"Never Say Never"

Charlie had finished laying a fresh set of towels on
the guest bed when he heard the front door open and
close. He listened for the creak of the old hardwoods
beneath Grae's heels, but it never came. Either she'd
changed her mind and stayed dripping on the porch, or
she was in his living room.

His brain begged to be released, to let his gifts work
their magic and seek his answers, but he kept a firm
hold on his abilities. He needed the distance between

them. It was the only way he'd be able to protect her and keep his heart intact.

"Hello?"

Her feeble question flooded his system with every protective instinct he possessed. He flung the feelings aside and poked his head into the hallway. Sure enough, she stood immediately inside the door, wet through to her skin. He attempted to look away from the soaked silk blouse that clung to her chest, but his all-male brain refused to comply.

When he felt her eyes on him, he called, "Down here. Thought you might need a few things." He ducked back into the guest room. His late mother's influence was evident in every bit of this room, from the crocheted blanket covering the bottom half of the bed, to the lace curtains in the windows. Never had it bothered him before, but knowing Grae would cross the threshold any second made him consider offering her his bed instead. Something about sharing this with her felt too personal. Too real. Too raw for his frayed sense of decorum when it came to her.

The thought fell to the floor when a barefooted Grae stepped in the room behind him.

"Wow." A tight laugh added to the tension. "Is this your mom's room? If so, I can sleep on the couch. Wait! I remember that blanket. She had it in your living room growing up. It always hung on the back of the couch. I think I even slept in it once when I was home sick from school and Mom had to go a few towns over to care for a woman delivering breech."

With a snap, he slung the afghan in question over his shoulder and slid around her, careful not to make contact. "No. Mom's never seen the room. Sleep here. Towels are on the bed, and I'm sure there are some clean clothes in the chest." He nodded toward the cedar hope chest and dashed through the doorway. "I'm down the hall on the right if you need anything," he reminded over his shoulder mid-retreat.

Without breaking his stride, Charlie burst through the closed door to the master bedroom and almost ran smack into Colin. A *naked* Colin.

"Dude! Knock much?"

"It's my house. My room, even."

Colin angled his head to the side and smiled. He was the size of a refrigerator in his human form. Tall, broad, and if Charlie was the kind of guy to be insecure based on size alone, their friendship wouldn't exist. But that all changed years ago, when Charlie had accepted the Wind Elemental living as the chocolate lab mooching table scraps. Unlike most Elementals, Colin hadn't grown up with people in the community. He'd bounced from foster home to foster home until his thirteenth birthday when the shapeshifting started. Afraid for his life, he'd committed to an animal form and made do until he wound up in Harmony about five years ago.

Now, his bared friend hid nothing. Charlie tossed the afghan in his hand at him. "Put something on."

"Sure. What'cha got that I can borrow?" He wrapped the blanket around his waist while he waited. "You didn't give me time to hide a go bag." Colin shrugged his shoulders and looked around the room.

"Yeah." Charlie offered a small smile and moved to his dresser. The top drawer had a few pairs of boxer briefs he'd never worn. Presents from Maureen, despite his insistence on going commando. He palmed a pair and tossed them in Colin's direction. "And I appreciate you coming so quick. I'm sure someone's after Grae. Something's not right, but I can't put my finger on it." He tossed the words over his shoulder as he shucked his wet clothes and put on a pair of sleep pants and a dry tee.

"Really? Why her?" Colin dropped the blanket, stepped into the boxers, and pulled them up his thighs. "Dude, these are mighty tight. How do you wear them all the time?"

"I don't." Charlie gave his friend a quick glance. The boxers did little to cover him. "Maybe I have some clean sweats around here."

"So you keep these ball crushers here as a gag?"

"Maureen bought them for me."

"Oh, shit. She's not gonna to take too kindly to you having Gracelynn here over night, is she?" Colin covered his mouth with his hand as he laughed.

"Shh…Grae doesn't know you're here." He pulled a mostly clean looking pair of sweats from a pile on his closet floor, sniffed it, and passed it along. "If Grae knew I'd asked you to come keep an eye on her…she'd be pissed and might bolt. It's bad enough that I have to take her in for questioning tomorrow." He shook his head.

"I get it." Colin answered after he removed the boxers and slid into the sweats. They were tight at his waist, but hung long on his legs. He clapped a hand on Charlie's shoulder and handed him the uncomfortable undergarment. "You want to protect her. But with the history between you, I'm surprised you even trust me in the same house with her."

"We don't have a history, really," Charlie insisted.

"Oh yeah?" Colin paced back over to the pooled heap of granny squared yarn and plucked it off the floor. "I heard you guys talking out there. QB didn't stand a chance. But I bet it had nothing to do with whatever he said *he* wanted to give her, and more to do with what *you* wanted to." Colin's eyebrows waggled as he pantomimed making out with the blanket.

Heat raced across Charlie's cheeks. "I didn't say that. And stop fucking with the blanket my mom made. It's damn creepy to watch."

Colin laughed his low rumble and tossed the blanket on the bed. "Dude, you didn't have to. Your face says it every time you look at her."

Outside the room, the squeak of worn floorboards telegraphed Grae's footsteps. She was on the move. Charlie touched his index finger to his lips and waved Colin into the far corner of the room so she wouldn't see him when Charlie opened the door. He tiptoed across the room and prayed the door hinges wouldn't squeal.

He half expected to see her still in her rain-wet clothes, slinking toward the front door, looking for her fuck-me heels, but he was wrong. Instead, she sported an old tee, one from his police academy days. Well-worn and thin, it clung to her curves like it was meant for her to wear. From his vantage point, he watched as she padded across the hall to the bathroom and reached her hand out in search of the light switch. When the lights sparked to life, evidence of her earlier claim was evident. Not a panty line to be found.

His mind wandered. Perhaps she boycotted body hair with the same enthusiasm as she refused underwear. The locking of the bathroom door and rush of water from the faucet shook him from his thoughts.

"Dude. That thing I was talking about earlier?" Colin hissed. "It's all over your face again." His teeth flashed with a knowing smile. "I'm gonna go patrol outside. Give you two a little alone time." He winked. "Just leave a window ajar." One more wink and his friend shifted from his human form into that of the chocolate lab, leaving Charlie's sweats in tatters.

The water stopped in the bathroom. He tossed a look Colin's way and yanked off the wet shirt. *Now or never.* Rethinking his choice at the last minute, he grabbed the granny square blanket that still smelled like home. A mix of floral perfume and baked apples wound around him as it landed on his shoulders. He patted his thigh and walked out into the hall.

"Come on, boy, I'll let you out," he called looking over his shoulder to ensure Colin took the hint.

When his chest crashed into Grae's side, he couldn't decide if the shocked look on her face was because of the collision, or the way their bodies seemed to meld together as if controlled by instinct.

"Sorry," they chorused in unison.

Grae stepped back first, to his disappointment, but the warmth of her body lingered on his skin.

"I see you found something to wear."

She fingered the hem of the tee and nodded, eyes not meeting his.

"Good. I didn't want you to spend the whole night wet."

A pink blush spilled over her chest, dashed up her throat, and raced across her cheeks before he blinked.

"Yeah. Thanks." She ducked around him and practically danced into the guest room. "'Night," she answered, cutting the light, and vaulting into the bed without closing the door.

Charlie passed a hand through his hair. She hadn't closed the door. Literally. It stood open between them. *Now or never.*

He motioned Colin toward the front door. Even in his canine form, Charlie could imagine his friend laughing an "I-told-you-so" jeer. Colin's tail wagged a little too happily as he trotted to the door and waited for Charlie open it.

The minute it took to release Colin from house and lock up behind him was the longest in Charlie's life. He passed by the kitchen and opened the window over the sink a crack. Later, Colin'd get in through the one inch opening in his natural Wind form. Thinking of his friend brought all the old memories Colin kept locked away to the front of Charlie's mind. He shook them away. Colin would be mortified to know Charlie had knowledge of his unhappy upbringing, so he kept quiet and pretended to know only what had been shared over the years.

A small moan reached his ears.

Now or never. It only took twenty-seven steps to move from the kitchen sink to the guest bedroom down the hall, but with every footfall, it felt too far.

He wrapped a hand around the doorjamb and leaned into the guest room. "Need anything?" A second ticked by without an answer, followed by another. His ears prickled when a soft sniffle broke the silence. "Grae? Everything okay?"

"Yeah."

Her whimper of a reply wouldn't convince even the most oblivious person on the planet. "Can I come in for a minute?"

He took her silence as consent and crossed the threshold. The room was dark but he could make out the shape of her curved body on the far side of the bed. Without asking permission, he dropped the blanket from his shoulders, crawled onto the unoccupied side of the bed, and moved so his hip bumped against her backside.

"Talk to me, Grae." He ran his hand over her hair, brushing it behind her ear so she couldn't hide her face.

Her breath hitched with a silent sob, and every ounce of his carefully crafted control caved. The block in his head disappeared. Grae must've lost the battle for control as well, because her thoughts flew fast and frenzied into his mind. Images of Sophie's dead body were the most overwhelming and reoccurring of them. So vivid and realistic, the coppery scent of her blood tainted the air surrounding them. The next set of images were Grae, frozen in place in the bar, the sound of the killer's thoughts playing at the edge of her subconscious. Yet her feet stayed planted, immobile. A glint of silver in the periphery of her vision, the tearing of her flesh. More blood. This time hers.

Her sobs grew louder.

"Shhh. I'm here. Nothing's going to hurt you. I'll protect you," he soothed against her temple as he drew her quaking body closer against him. Her heart echoed against her ribs and reverberated along his arms, bonding them in the moment.

She mourned her mother. A loss so deep and dark, he felt her falling. A fall he was all too familiar with. He rolled away from her only long enough to grab the blanket his mother had made. With a shaky breath, he wrapped it around their entwined bodies. They were safe, tucked beneath the warm yarn, holding onto each other as if their lives depended on it. He placed a chaste kiss against Grae's temple and pulled her even closer.

"I won't let anything happen to you. If ever I could promise you something, it's this: I'll protect you with the last breath in my body, Gracelynn George. I promise you that."

11

Random Thought # 52 - Silver linings are a fraud made up by optimists to encourage more optimism.

Gracelynn's shirt clung to her body, held tight by the sticky sweat from the warmth of her bed. Wait. Not her bed. She wasn't in North Carolina. She was in New Jersey. And not in her childhood home, either.

A puff of warm air tickled the back of her neck, reminding her not only where she was, but also who had his arm wrapped around her body.

Wide awake, she searched her brain for a *Plan B.* Lying in bed beside Charlie didn't bode well as a *Plan A.* Instead, it reeked of problem-causing, and her problems already exceeded her coping capacity. Someone wanted her dead. Her mom was already dead—presumably because she was trying to protect Grae. The title of *prime suspect* likely belonged squarely on her shoulders as far as the cops were concerned. And, if she remembered correctly, she'd practically thrown herself at the man spooning her.

Yup. She needed an escape hatch from her current predicament, the one that could include getting caught snuggling with the hottest cop in town. A cop who not only read her mind, but had once kissed her senseless and never looked back. The same guy who'd spent a good portion her younger years dancing through her dreams would have to take her in for questioning, and potentially stand there to formally accuse her of her mother's murder.

Her heart flip flopped, missing a beat. With her mom dead, who would help her get rid of the voices? She rolled out from under the weight of Charlie's arm and sat on the edge of the bed. A deep breath and a drink of water, that was what she needed. She took the deep breath, and another for good measure and then made her way through the house. The kitchen was small, but practical. A clock on the oven indicated the sun would rise soon, meaning it was already a brand-new day.

Rather than search through the cabinets, she opted for a black coffee mug hanging from a peg on the wall. She rinsed the mug and caught the scrawl of letters written on it by the low light Charlie must've left on so she could find her way around.

Cops Do It In Handcuffs.

For the first time since running into Charlie at the bar, she laughed. She filled the mug from the tap and sat at the small table in the corner. From her new vantage point, she saw all the mugs had similar humorous sayings on them. She shook her head and smiled, her stress fading away with the seconds ticking on the clock. He still surprised her when she least expected it.

She set the mug on the table and stretched.

"Oh. Sorry. I thought you were Charlie," a low, gravelly voice whispered.

Gracelynn sprang from her seat, nearly knocking over the chair. "Who the hell are you?" She eyed the man in question. He was easily over six foot, but broader than most men, with abs that begged a woman to wash their lingerie on them. His dark hair was cut close, military-style close, and his dark eyes were fixed on her. He wore the tightest pair of boxers she'd ever seen on a man. Self-conscious, she pulled the fabric of Charlie's tee away from her chest and wound her arms in an awkward shield in front of her.

"I'm…" he trailed off with a mumble and looked away, as if unable to hold her gaze.

His mumbled words missed her ears. "Who?" She opened her mind and plucked the answer straight from his brain. Too bad the answer had little to do with his name and more to do with his job. "My babysitter? Are you freaking kidding me?" Annoyed, she snatched the mug off the table and waved it at the man as if scolding him. "Are you a detective too? I didn't kill my mother. And I wasn't planning on running away. Fucking Charlie. Bastard." The last word came from under her breath, but she meant it all the same. She set the mug in the sink with a bang and pushed her index finger into the guy's rock hard chest.

"Might as well cuff me now. Lest, I try to run." Sarcasm coated every syllable and she punctuated her demand with an eye roll. She then pulled her finger back and raised her hands together in surrender.

"Oh, shit."

Gracelynn turned at Charlie's expletive and sighed as his hard muscles flexed when he ran a hand through his sleep-ruffled hair. *Damn.* He looked good. Somewhere in the back of her brain she caught a whiff of his thoughts, and not a single one was anything other than complimentary about the way his shirt looked on her. She bit back a smug smile and tried to focus on the situation at hand.

"So you didn't trust me after all?" The nonchalance of her question surprised even her.

"It's not that." He ran a hand through his hair again.

She heard his mental *shit* run through her head with the gesture. Charlie unnerved? She never believed it a possibility.

"I'm not a cop," piped up the almost naked guy. "Really. Pinky swear." He offered the aforementioned digit on his right hand.

"Yeah, Colin's not a cop."

"Hell, no," he agreed. "Not that there's anything wrong with being a cop," he added, a look of chagrin on his face.

"What are you doing here then?" She directed the question at Colin, and held up a hand to stop Charlie when he opened his mouth to answer.

"Honestly?" Colin glanced in Charlie's direction before continuing.

"Don't ask him. Just answer the question. Why are you here?"

Colin tapped the tops of his fingers on both hands against his thumbs. She recognized the nervous tick for what it was and switched from her demanding tone into her therapist mode. "Look, I get it. You're in a tough spot. It's obvious you and Charlie are close..." A weird image shot through her brain at the words. Charlie and the chocolate lab from earlier. Ah... Knowing what she did about the Elemental Community, the pieces of the puzzle began to fall into place.

"I guess I should properly thank you for the situation with the bobcat," she continued. "How's your ass feeling after the bite?"

"Not too bad. I heal pretty quickly after I shift. In fact, your mom was the one who helped me understand my gift. A good number of Winds shift like I do. Not so many can choose their form, though."

A heavy silence hung in the room. Colin realized his mistake about thirty seconds too late by Gracelynn's estimate.

"Dude." Charlie's chastisement came with a swift smack on the back of Colin's head. "Too soon."

"No, it's okay," she argued, before turning her attention back to Colin. "So you aren't a cop. You're the dog who saved our butts out there. But that doesn't explain why you're here."

She reached a hand out and guided him to a chair at the kitchen table. "Look, I don't know what Charlie's told you, but let me be clear. I didn't kill my mom. Like you, I came back to Harmony for her help." She let her revelation wash over him before she continued. "I'm sure you've heard the rumors about me anyway, so I've got nothing to gain by lying to you. Especially since I kinda owe you one for the bobcat thing." The smile on her lips was perfectly practiced from years of speaking with her clients. "It's true I'm a half. My mom is a Wind, much like you, but my dad was human." She settled in the chair opposite him and fiddled with her fingers on the table.

"So pure-bloods can have kids with non-pure-bloods?" His dark grey eyes turned stormy.

Unable to help herself, Gracelynn dipped into his thoughts and found his brain already full since Charlie's mental footprint took up residence as well. The shifter's thoughts were fuzzy, blurred, disconnected.

"Yes," she answered and shot Charlie a glare. "Why do you ask? Is there a human girl in your life?"

Charlie visibly startled and Colin rubbed his hands against his eyes as if trying to clear his vision.

"I don't know," he admitted. "Have you ever had a weird feeling about something that you couldn't put your finger on?"

"Sure. It's kinda how I felt on my last birthday, when I started hearing things in my head." The words tumbled out honestly and she wished she could retract every single one. "I mean…" She searched for a way to cover up her admission. "Being part of this magical community definitely causes confusion."

Colin watched her carefully, but Charlie ignored them both and went to the cupboard. He removed a small tin like she'd seen in her mom's apothecary and lifted the lid. As soon as the fragrant leaves were steeped in the hot water, a familiar scent wafted through the kitchen. The complicated aroma called forth the memory of her mom, as this was the same tea she drank daily.

"It's more than that. At least, I think it is. I've spoken to Elms about it, and she was going to talk to your mom about seeing me. Elms was heading there tonight." Colin's voice dropped an octave and his head fell forward as he pulled her from her thoughts. "I'm so sorry, Gracie. Charlie asked me to come keep an eye on you. I don't know if you know what he can do, but he called me and said he thought he heard someone thinking about killing you. I know our boy isn't the emotionally open type, but he was worried about you." He stopped talking long enough to cast an apologetic shrug in Charlie's direction. "He'll probably kick my ass for telling you, but you've been through enough already tonight. So think of me as your incognito bodyguard. Okay?"

Unable to restrain the emotion welling in her chest, Gracelynn launched from her seat and threw herself at Colin, enveloping him in a bear hug.

"Thank you for everything." She buried her face in his chest as tears fell. Someone who was open and honest in this community needed to be treasured.

"I didn't do anything," he protested, wrapping his strong arms around her shaking body. "Really. It was all Charlie. He called me."

"Charlie's gonna go back to bed," Charlie muttered as he replaced the tin and marched from the kitchen.

A thread of his thoughts trickled into Gracelynn's mind. Somber and sedate, her chest felt heavy with emotion belonging to him. She pulled herself from Colin's embrace and darted across the kitchen. A light breeze brushed past her as Colin left in his Elemental form. Just as Charlie was about to pass the guest room, she brushed his shoulder with her fingertips.

"Please, wait. I think I owe you an apology."

He cut her off. "No apologies needed, Grae."

She scooted in front of him and stood firm. "Did you really ask Colin to come protect me?" She watched in the darkness for any signs of deception or avoidance, but none came.

"You did," she confirmed from his silence. "Thank you." She ducked her head against the onslaught of words threatening to pour from her mouth.

"Don't. Please? Share whatever you're thinking."

"It's not like you don't already know."

"You're better at guarding than I am," he confided. "But I can tell something is trying to get out. Please, Grae?"

"You protected me. And instead of being grateful, I tried to figure out how you were going to manipulate me into confessing to Mom's murder. I didn't trust you, and I should've."

"Look, you trusted me before, and I screwed it up. It only makes sense that now you might not trust me." He smoothed her hair back from her face, tucking it behind her ear. "I made a lot of mistakes where you were concerned when we were younger, but there's no way I could let you get hurt. Not then, and sure as hell not now."

She sighed, relishing the heat of his hand so close to her face. Without her consent, her body melted into him. And not just a little. Her traitorous self full-on pressed against him, soaking in his strength, and basking in the light scent of sandalwood that lingered on his skin.

"If anyone owes someone an apology, it's me," he whispered against her temple. "I should've been stronger back then."

"Hush," she scolded and met his eyes. "I've thought about that night more times than I should over the years." The confession sent a rush of heat scorching through her veins. When the dull ache in her chest released, a wave of freedom washed over her. Freedom from her past, from her new gifts, from the restraint she clung to around Charlie Latham.

"I'm so sorry, Grae. I never should've overstepped like that. You were young and so innocent. I should've been the adult—"

She refused to listen to him take back that magical moment. A surge of boldness swelled in her gut. She flicked her tongue across her lips and rose to her toes to plant a kiss on his mouth, effectively silencing him.

Satisfaction coursed through her when their tongues tangled together and he wound his fingers into her hair, tugging her closer. She slid her hands up his bare chest and toyed with the ridges and valleys as his muscles flexed. She skimmed her way to his shoulders and leaned closer into him. Air froze in her lungs as his hands moved to her backside.

"I need you," she panted when they parted for a brief second. "Please!"

Without a word, Charlie hitched her up against his chest and carried her into the guest room. Her legs wrapped around his waist as his mouth found hers, and a feeling of 'home' blistered in both her head and her heart.

They crossed the threshold and he stopped. A train of uncertainty ran through her mind. "Don't stop now," she begged.

"Grae."

A sharp shake of her head answered his protest. "We're consenting adults. And I know if you look, you'll see I've wanted this for a long time." She slid her hands into his hair and laid her forehead against his. "See for yourself," she panted, her heartbeat spiking as his erection throbbed against her uncovered core, only the fabric of his pants separating them.

She felt the brush of his mind against hers and waited for him to find the answers he needed. Seconds later, her confidence jumped as he hardened further against her heat. This was it. She was finally going to know what it was like to be loved by the one and only Charlie Latham. The smile fastened on her face threatened to flow into a stream of word vomit professing her long hidden feelings, but she managed to construct a mental dam in time to keep him from finding them in her head.

She kicked the guest room's door closed as he carried her to the bed and moaned deep in her throat. Silver linings sparkled after all.

*Random Thought # 23 - When rational thought
fails, consequences are doubled.*

Grae's lack of underwear drove him nuts, and the
need to rip his shirt off her body built at a furious
pace. He'd been a gentleman far too long where she
was concerned.

A little voice in the back of his head sounded, reminding him to take the proper precautions, but he
quieted it without debate. Because of Sophie's help,
bonding wasn't an option for him. He'd seen the dark
side of the curse his people clung to like a lifeline. Fated mates, his ass. His parents believed that nonsense

and look where it landed them—in matching graves. A process that determined which two people spent the rest of their lives together wasn't a notion he could get behind.

People like Sophie George, who bucked the system and turned away their fated mates, lived longer, happier lives. Look at her daughter. Sure, she'd struggled at times, but she'd had a home and a mother who loved her without question. He could have that. All he needed to do was stay the course and make sure these moments with Grae were about her, and not his own burning need.

Years of memories flashed before his eyes as he struggled to keep his control: Grae's first broken bone. Her first date. The time she went to his senior prom with that jerk from the soccer team. The tears that streamed down her face when he'd found her in the back hallway, her dress ripped. The way she'd looked in the moonlight as he 'd driven her around for hours until she'd finally told him what had happened.

He'd let her down too that night. He'd only meant to kiss away her tears, but something about seeing her so sad made kissing her lips seem like the right thing to do. To prove to her not all men were jerks. It wasn't the first time he'd kissed her after all, and hell, it'd felt so right...

And here he was, folding her in his arms, with nothing stopping him. No bobcats, no tear-stained faces, no damn underwear.

She moaned and pushed her breasts against his chest. Her arched back presented the hollow of her throat to his mouth. Temptation won out. He swirled his tongue against her skin, hoping to hear the heavenly sound of her moan again. She rewarded him with more than he could've imagined. *Fuck it,* ran through his head in his own voice. There was no chance they'd bond. The community had its ideals about pure-bloods mating, but he had an inkling they were wrong. And this one indiscretion wouldn't be the thing that was going to change their lives. Besides, if giving her this would provide the comfort she needed, he'd gladly make the sacrifice.

"Don't make me beg," she panted in his ear. "I've been waiting ten years for this moment."

Grae released his hair and raked her nails down his chest, leaving little bites of pain in her wake.

"You'll be the death of me if you keep that up." He growled and took the remaining steps to the bed. Instead of dropping her to the mattress, he twisted and took the brunt of the impact, strategically nestling his cock at her core. He clung to her back and pressed against her. Heat stoked his passion. "Take off the shirt," he commanded.

She smiled in his embrace and he released his unyielding grip.

Rising to her knees like a goddess, she smiled. "All you had to do was ask." She stroked her fingers down her body until they landed at the hem of the shirt.

His attention pulsed between the budding of her nipples beneath the fabric, and the micro movements her hands made as she inched the shirt up her abdomen. His hands itched to grab the fabric, rip it from her body and ball it tight, but a piece of him relished the slow torturous show she put on.

A wicked smile played across her lips. Patience parted ways with reason. He lunged at one of the waiting peaks and sucked it through the thin cotton. Her surprised shriek spurred him on. When her fingers rooted deep against his scalp again, he released the taut bud and spoke, "I want to taste every inch of you."

She scrambled to pull the shirt over her head, revealing her beautiful body to him.

"You like that idea, don't you?" He rubbed his unshaven face between her breasts gently until she gasped.

"Protection?" She pushed him into the mattress and rose enough to slide her hand into the waistband of his fleece sleep pants. She freed his cock though the unbuttoned fly.

"I have some in my room," he answered, the heat of her only hardening him more.

"Are you clean?"

"Yes." He never considered sex without protection. Not only did it reduce his risk of disease, it took out the mixing of fluids that could start the bonding process. He wasn't stupid.

"Me too," she agreed, before adding, "I'm on the pill anyway."

Warm, wet walls of her womanhood surrounded him before his brain understood her previous words. "Fuuuuuuuuck." She rose and dipped in rhythm of their joined heartbeats, her head tossed back, eyes closed. She was a goddess. *His* goddess. He drank his fill of her before palming her breasts in his hands and lifting his hips to meet her thrusts.

She rode him hard and unbridled. Digging her heels into his thighs as he felt her tighten against the oncoming orgasm. She bucked as her inner walls held him, pulsating with passion.

"Ohmygosh." The words fell from her lips and replayed over and over again as she drew him over the edge with her.

"Grae!"

JENI BURNS

Her name slipped out before he could lock it inside. Hungry for more of her, he claimed her breast with his mouth, sending a fresh wave of ripples through him and around his manhood. His own name hit his ears as she crested the peak into ecstasy again. Something deep inside him savored the sound. Every syllable a stamp of approval he never knew he'd been craving. He closed his eyes and images assaulted his mind. A thin gold thread wrapped around his heart, found its way to hers, and claimed it as his.

Tied together.
Bound forever.
Oh, shit.

13

Random Thought # 591 - Long lasting love was created by greeting card companies.

Gracelynn felt the not-so-subtle-shift in Charlie's demeanor soon after she yelled his name. Sure, he'd done the same thing moments prior, but for some reason, he seemed upset when she'd called his out. She opened her mind to his and was greeted with a surge of panic, deep-seated to his core.

Fantastic. Just what she needed. Another rejection. She slid off his lap and snagged the discarded shirt as she marched across the hall to the bathroom. She didn't bother covering herself for the short walk, but wished she had when she ran into Colin coming out of the bathroom.

"Sorry, Gracie!" he exclaimed and did his best to keep his eyes at the top of her head.

They danced in the hall, each trying to move out of the other's way.

"Stop," she finally begged, desperate for a door to put between her and the rest of the world. Colin stood statue still, and she brushed past him into the tile and marble-filled sanctuary.

Charlie's footsteps echoed on the hardwoods as she closed the door and clicked the locked into place. Resting her back against the door, she heard Charlie and Colin's muted voices outside.

"Dude, she looked upset. What did you do?"

"Nothing," Charlie snapped. "Where is she?"

"In there."

Silence hung heavy inside the bathroom and out.

"Am I supposed to be protecting her from you too?"

Floorboards creaked under what she assumed were Colin's feet.

"What?"

"It just looks to me like maybe you took advantage…"

She imagined her protector attempting to intimidate his friend. Ridiculous. Being here caused too many problems. She wished she could rewind time and never agree to come back to Harmony with her mom.

"Oh, hell. It wasn't like that."

Hearing Charlie sound so dejected hurt even more.

"Then why do you both look so damn upset?"

"I fucked things up. I didn't stop to think, and now we're completely screwed."

Gracelynn refused to listen to anymore backpedaling and regrets. She threw the shirt on the floor, stepped into the glass enclosed shower, and turned on the water. The cold spray did little to soothe her bruised ego. What had she been thinking? The guy she'd dreamed about for the greater part of her life finally showed an interest, so she...*what*...Jumped on him? Took advantage of his kindness and understanding? Took advantage of his body? Damn. She was awful.

She cranked the water temperature hotter until the droplets fell like burning embers on her skin. Hoping the water could cleanse her of every awful decision she'd ever made, she scrubbed until her skin ached and her scalp screamed for mercy. Only then did she shut off the water and step into the steamy room.

Wrapping herself in a towel, she took a deep breath and prepared herself for what was to come. She saw the first rays of sunlight through the window and squared her shoulders.

Opening the door pained her, because on the other side, there was nothing to greet her but emptiness. She should've expected it, but still it gave her a pang right near her heart. Oh, well. The distance between where she stood and her clothes wasn't far, but her legs dragged as if walking through wet sand, and her heart hung like a lead balloon in her chest.

Her clothes sat, neatly folded, on the dresser. They were still slightly damp from the storm the night before, but she wiggled into them. Feeling raw, she craved anything to help her situation, but after searching the room for her heels, she came up empty. *That's right.* She'd taken them off at the front door. Years of living in an old home with beautiful hardwoods dictated the habit of removing heels upon entering so as to not pock the floors.

Her resolve intact, she moved through the seemingly empty house. A niggling sense tickled at the back of her mind. Sure, Charlie was feeling regret, but would he actually leave his own home to get away from the reminder of their tryst? And what about Colin? He left her with the impression he'd be wherever she was. She stopped by the door and stepped into the one heel that stood where she'd left it. The other one had disappeared apparently. She kicked the first one off and dropped to her knees to check under the couch.

To catch a rat, you only need the right bait.

The words chilled her to the core. Once her heart got the memo to keep beating, she rushed to her feet, ready for anything. She swung around and found a uniformed policeman standing before her, an odd look on his face.

"Oh! Sorry officer, you scared me." Gracelynn drew back a step, putting distance between them. "Are you here to drive Charlie and me to the station?"

His lips twisted into a sneer. "Charlie had to run out. I'll take you in myself."

"Oh. Okay... I just need to find my other heel. It was here last night."

"Maybe his dog chewed it up," the officer suggested.

The idea of Colin eating one of her heels... Insane. Gracelynn inspected the man closer. The badge on his chest looked real enough, but how would she really *know*. Plus, his stance was all wrong. Aggressive. Dominant. Overpowering. And he wasn't even a big guy.

She took a breath and opened her mind. The thoughts that tumbled through terrified her. He was, in fact, a cop.

He was also a killer.

Her heart skyrocketed as snippets of a conversation played through his mind. How easy tricking Charlie had been. The fake call about a body deep in the woods would keep him gone for hours. And the unexpected animal who had greeted him at the door, now lay asleep on the front porch, thanks to the Valium stash in the police officer's pocket.

Gracelynn embraced her gift and sought the human piece of Colin's mind she felt in his animal form the night before, but the only brain pattern she found was the officer's.

"Don't worry about your shoe. We need to get you down to the station. The chief wants to personally question you."

"Sure, but it's cold out there and I need something on my feet," she protested, still trying to maintain the appearance of cooperation. If there was one thing she knew after years of counseling people, it was that women who acted as a damsel in distress were often treated as such and underestimated. If she could convince this guy she was harmless, maybe he'd let his guard down and she could make a break for it.

She dropped to her knees again. Her missing heel was wedged under a bookshelf. She'd crawled over to it when the officer's appreciation of her ass wafted through her head.

"So where did Charlie go?" She took her time removing her shoe from its spot.

"Crime scene."

"Oh, that's awful. Not another dead person, I hope. I can't get the sight of my poor mom in a pool of blood out of my head." Her words were meant to disarm her wannabe attacker, but they were true nonetheless. "Is it another woman? I saw in the paper there seems to be someone targeting women. Should I be scared?"

"No. I'm sure you'll be safe. Of course, that's assuming you're innocent."

She put her shoes on and rose to her feet, the trembling in her limbs authentic. "I didn't kill anyone. I only came to visit my mom, and now she's gone." As the tears rolled down her cheeks, she could feel the officer's heart softening. "I wish I'd spent more time with her and less time so far away," she sobbed. "I can't believe I was such an awful daughter. I always thought we'd fix things later. And now look..." She spread her hands in front of her for emphasis. "Now it's too late. I'll never hear her voice again. We'll never repaint that awful mailbox. And I'll never get to tell her she was a good mom even though I didn't always say it."

She hurried to the couch and flopped onto it, her body quaking.

"I'm sure your mom knew you loved her," the officer interjected, surprising her with his tender tone.

"No. I was such a difficult kid. Always wanting more than she could give." She dropped her head into her hands as the hiccups started.

"Here, let me get you a glass of water," the man offered and ducked from the room.

This was her chance. She snatched off her shoes, holding them in one hand while she grabbed her clutch from the chair with the other, and snuck out the front door. The grass was cool beneath her feet, but she didn't stop. She ran as if the devil was on her heels waiting to drag her into Hell. It wasn't until she reached the edge of the river that she realized her mistake. She should've run towards the woods. There, she could've hid, but no—

WIND'S SOLACE

Without thinking anything further, she'd instinctively run toward the water. All those years spending time in the Delaware River gave her a false sense of security in its presence. Uncertain if her captor was aware of her disappearing act, she did the only thing she could rationalize and plunged her feet into the cold waves lapping the shore.

Her knees knocked and her joints ached as she submerged herself. Taking a deep breath, she sank under the water. She needed to get away as fast as she could.

She considered the stony river bed below her and wondered if this would be how she died—hitting her head on an unseen rock in the current while someone on shore waited with a gun. *Damn.*

As her body begged for air, she willed herself to stay submerged. She closed her mind and she noticed a shift in her body, as if it was slowly becoming one with the traveling current. Her skin no longer felt the cold. Her lungs no longer throbbed. Her arms and legs no longer propelled her forward.

It was as if she'd done the unthinkable and embraced the water as her own, becoming one with it. Without time to contemplate, she tuned her senses into the areas she passed through until she could taste the concrete and steel of the bridge downstream from Harmony.

Uncertain how to pull herself together, she began to panic. The rapid fire beating in her chest led to her depleted lungs screaming for air, and helped engage her limbs so she could kick to the surface. The first mouthful of air was the sweetest she'd ever breathed.

Fighting the current, she swam to the shore near a small park. As she waded through the deeper parts, the tug of waves pulsed against her thighs. Yup, she was missing something. The same somethings which the lack of would get her noticed, since she was as naked as the day was long. Her shoes and handbag were likely somewhere at the bottom of the river, along with her clothes and dignity.

She swam farther downstream. A mile or so later, she spied an encampment of sorts. She dragged her tired body from the water and shivered in the cold air.

"Look 'ver there, Smitty. It's a lady. A neked one!"

"She's all wet, Tony. Must've had an accident in the river. You got an extra coat?"

"It's my dead-of-winter one. I'll need it back."

"I'm sure a lady like her would give it back once her mess is all sorted out."

Gracelynn shivered against the cold and tried to stop her jaw from shaking long enough to promise the men, who appeared to be living in this makeshift homeless camp, that she'd return the coat.

"Here, honey, wrap yourself in this here coat. It's not the cleanest, but it's warm."

The man named Tony offered her an old winter coat with only half of its original stuffing inside, but when she slipped it over herself, it warmed her. The other man gently took her arm and guided her toward a trashcan they used as a heat source. Finally, the blood began to flow through her veins and carry the warmth of the coat with it. She could almost think straight. Well, at least straight enough to determine neither man had nefarious intentions toward her. She placed her hands over the edge of the bin and relished the warmth.

"Thank you." She managed the words without her teeth clattering.

"Are you okay, miss?"

She looked deep into the older man's weather-worn face and mustered up a smile.

"I think so. Just a bad fall into the water. Remembered something about clothes weighing you down and causing drownings..." She nodded as she spoke and hoped they bought her story. Because the reality might get her locked in a psych ward.

"Well, you warm up here, and I'll see if we can scrounge up something for you to eat. It's a bit early for even the pantries to be open yet, but I might have a little something tucked away."

She watched as the men strode, shoulder to shoulder, toward two small old tents. At a loss, she tried to stop tears banging on her eyelids, but even with all her resolve gathered, she was hopeless. Her phone was in her purse somewhere at the bottom of the river, and the only person locally whose number she knew off the top of her head was dead.

The tears flowed without restraint.

"Aww, don't'cha worry, sweetie."

Startled, she turned and faced a woman with crooked teeth and a weary smile. She must've been about sixty.

"There's places people like us can go that can help. But in the meantime, I might have some pants you can fit." She waved Gracelynn to follow as she made her way between the tents. When they arrived at an old army green tarp fastened with bricks and a sturdy tree branch, the woman sank to her knees and crawled under the rough plastic. The multitude of emotions running through Gracelynn overflowed when she returned with not only a pair of sweatpants, but also a sweatshirt.

"Here ya go. Should keep you warm enough until we can get you to the mission." She twirled her finger in the air in a 'turn around' gesture and added, "Go ahead, put them on. Ain't no one looking."

Gracelynn did as told. The material was worn, but the softness warmed her and her gratitude overflowed much like her tears had.

"Does anyone know where you are, sweetie? Can we help you get back to where you belong? I can tell you aren't like us. You look too soft to have lived on the streets." She tucked a wayward strand of hair behind Gracelynn's ear. "There's a lady down at the church on 9th Street who's married to a police officer. She's helped a lot of people find their way back home."

"No police." Her voice shook. Unsure where she was, she didn't want to risk the officer from Charlie's finding her. Her face must've shown her panic, because the woman put both hands up in an 'I surrender' gesture before saying anything more.

"Okay. We don't have to call the police. But we should get you some clothes and a meal."

"Grae? Grae! Where are you? Answer me if you can hear me, damn it!"

Charlie's voice sounded loud and clear in her head. So much so, that she swung her head around trying to locate where it came from.

"Charlie?"

"Who's Charlie, sweetie?"

"Where the hell are you? I just got a call that you vanished. I'm headed back toward the house."

"How am I hearing you right now?" She rubbed her temples and realized belatedly she'd spoken aloud again.

"Sweetie, I think maybe we should get you to the church. They have doctors they can call if you are out of your medication. Smitty used to fly off the rocker sometimes before the docs were able to get him some pills. Is that why you're all out of sorts? Did you wander off without your pills?"

The earnest look on the woman's face warmed her heart. Charlie would save her, but until then, this woman seemed content to ensure her well-being.

She met the woman's gaze and smiled. "I'm sorry. I think the cold water affected me more than I initially thought. Charlie's my boyfriend," she lied. "I don't know how I wound up in the water, but I'm sure he will come looking for me. Where am I, anyway?" She tried her best to arrange her features into something believable.

"Boyfriend? Oh, shit, Grae. You too? I thought maybe I made a mistake. Damn. I'm so sorry."

She didn't have time to concentrate on Charlie's words when the woman in front of her was insistent on talking.

"Why, sweetie, you're in Easton. Where are you supposed to be?"

"I was staying with Charlie..." She trailed off, debating how honest to be with the woman.

"Easton is only fifteen minutes out. Where in Easton?"

"I don't know," she mentally snapped.

"You mentioned a church. Can we go there? I'm feeling a bit hungry."

"All right, sweetie. I'll tell Smitty and Tony. They'll wanna get a hot meal too." The woman hurried off to where the men's tents were.

"Can you hear me?" She made sure this time to keep the communication completely in her mind.

"Loud and clear. Where are you?"

"I'm not sure. A homeless encampment on the river. South of the bridge, I think. Where are you?"

"I was called out to a supposed murder scene in Alpha, but there wasn't anything there. Why did you leave the house? I sent my old partner, Roy, and another officer out to watch over you."

"Well, one of them wanted to kill me."

"No way, that's not possible. Roy and I were partners for years. He'd never do something like that."

"Not sure who it was. I only saw one guy. Heard in his head that he'd tricked you into leaving and drugged Colin, who he thought was your dog. But I never got any indicators that he had someone else there with him."

"Oh, shit. Roy was the one who called me saying you fled the scene. I can't believe he'd be behind any of this though."

"Sweetie, let's head on over to the church. Get in line for something warm to set you straight until your boy can come for you." The woman placed her hand on Gracelynn's shoulder and steered her away from the river.

Her feet hurt on the small stones and she wanted to cry out, but held back. Knowing Charlie wasn't far gave her the strength she needed to keep moving forward. With every new turn they took, she mentally sent him descriptions of what she passed and street signs. And with each passing moment, he reassured her he was closing in.

By the time they made their way into the main streets of the city, she could hear Charlie's heartbeat in her head when he was silent. Her body quaked with anticipation, despite her current predicament. Something had shifted and she refused to consider what caused these feelings while knowing Charlie could hear every thought. But every time she closed her eyes, she sensed whatever connected them wrapped tighter around her.

Before they crossed Northampton Street, she felt Charlie's heated gaze on her. She stopped moving forward and turned. Sure enough, there he was, with his hands clenched around the steering wheel of his truck.

His anger brushed against her brain. *"What did they do to you?"*

"Charlie." His name was a sigh of relief on her lips.

"What, sweetie?"

"Charlie. He's here. Thank you for everything. I promise to repay you and bring you replacement clothes as soon as I can." She clasped the woman's hands. "Thank you for everything."

Charlie's door slammed closed and his boots scraped the ground as he ran to her.

"Is this your Charlie?" The woman's eyes brightened as his arm slipped around Gracelynn's shoulder.

"Yes, ma'am." He nodded. "I'm all hers."

His words stroked a tender spot in her heart.

"I can't thank you enough for taking care of her, *Miss...*"

"Call me Dot," she answered. "Is she okay? She was buck naked when she came out of the water and seemed pretty confused."

"She's had a rough few days, Dot. Her mother died suddenly and she's in shock. But I promise to take good care of her." He hugged her closer with his words and his genuine concern for her well-being whispered over her skin and sank deep into her pores.

"Thank you, Dot. I promise to repay you."

Charlie reached into his back pocket and pulled out his wallet, then removed a few crisp bills from the folds. "Please take this and use it to get yourself something warm to wear," he suggested offering her the money.

Gracelynn watched the play of emotions wash across the woman's face as she hesitated.

"That's not necessary." She shook her head and began to follow where Tony and Smitty had gone.

"Dot," Gracelynn called. "Please wait." She hurried on her sore feet to the woman's side. "Take it. Share it with them," she angled her chin toward the men. "Please. I'm not sure how soon I can get back here to repay you. I'll feel better knowing you have this in the meantime."

The woman took the cash and nodded. "Be good to yourself, sweetie. And don't let anyone steal your happiness."

The conspiratorial wink following her declaration made Gracelynn smile. Life could be funny sometimes.

"Let's get you home," Charlie whispered in her ear as he slid his arm around her shoulders and held her close.

Something in her heart changed at the contact. Irrevocably *his*. Her stomach sank. Her life would never again be the same.

Fuck.

14

Random Thought # 347 - My life didn't start until you, and now you, and only you, have the power to end it.

Her body pressing into his did little to relieve the worry churning in his gut. He needed to hear every word straight in her own voice, almost as much as he needed to kiss her. The second need overtook the first, and his lips found hers without a breath between for thought. She was cold beneath his touch, but the spark between them warmed him through.

He fought reality, withdrew from her, and aimed to put a respectable distance between them. He needed to regain control of his shit.

"What was that for?" Grae raised her brow and shivered as she touched her fingertips to her mouth.

The damn shiver nearly undid him. "Come on, let's get in the truck and get you warmed up." His hands itched to touch her again, but insecurity made him rethink it. Instead, he opted for opening her door and stepping back when she climbed into the truck.

"Please don't take me back to your place." Her teeth chattered, and she slunk down in the seat.

Charlie closed the door, gathered his wits, and jogged over to the driver's side. His heart clanged from the small distance separating them. The urge to vault into the cab and bear hug her almost overwhelmed him. He clenched his hands into fists and waited a beat before getting inside.

"So do you know who he was?"

Her headshake spurred him on.

"Did you get a good look?" He waited through her silence as she traced the lines of the tattoo on her left wrist. When she wound her index finger over the scripted image for the third time, he broke his silence. "I promised you last night, and I'll do it again, I won't let anything hurt you." The resounding thud in his chest echoed the sentiment. "I should never have left this morning. I thought there was another body, and I didn't want to miss anything in the case, especially if it can prove your innocence." He scratched the back of his head and avoided looking directly at her. "Besides, Colin was there, right?"

Moisture pooled in her eyes and she sank further into the leather seat. "Whoever that man was, he poisoned him. Or tried to, maybe. I don't know." Sobs heaved inner chest. "I didn't even see Colin when I ran out of there. Maybe he's dead."

Charlie's restraint broke. He reached over the center console and grabbed her hands in his. "Colin is resilient. If you only knew all he's been through, you wouldn't worry so much." His heart shattered. Never had it felt so important to reassure anyone. *Shit.*

Grae disengaged their entwined hands and swiped at her tears, while Charlie attempted to calm the storm brewing inside at the emptiness of his hand. He was screwed.

He gripped the wheel. Hard. His knuckles popping under the pressure as her remembered images assaulted his brain. He couldn't take her home, it wasn't safe anymore. If her memory was accurate, he recognized the potential attacker. Someone he trusted. And up until moments ago, would've trusted to keep Grae safe. *Shit.*

He shifted the truck into drive and pulled away from the curb. He needed an idea and fast, if he hoped for any chance of keeping her safe. He took the center circle of downtown Easton faster than posted and headed back to Jersey. Isaac would know what to do.

Gas pedal pushed to the floor, he hit the switch for the lightbar on top of his unmarked truck and swerved around everyone who was in his way.

"Can you slow down?"

Her voice quivered as he barreled past a semi hauling logs down Rt. 519.

"Can't. I've got to get you to Isaac's." He didn't spare a second to even glance in her direction as he skidded around the turn leading to where Isaac lived.

"Why there? Won't they think to look there? I mean he lives next door to…" Her words dropped into nothingness.

"I know. But as far as the rest of the world is concerned, Isaac is just your neighbor. No important connection between you two." He ground his molars until the tension in his jaw pained him. "And I can't take you into the station now."

"So the cop that was at your house is a real officer?"

"More than an officer. He was my fucking partner once." Anger spurred him faster around the curves in the road until the tires slid on some loose gravel.

"Charlie! Please, slow down!" Her hand grabbed his thigh with a vise grip. "That man was your partner? Does he know about us?"

"*Us?*" He choked against a lump lodged in his throat. How could Roy know he and Grae had bonded?

"Yeah." She removed her hand from his thigh and her tone changed to one of disgusted anger. "Look. I know I'm not a full Elemental like you, but I'm still enough of one to be lumped into the community, aren't I?"

Her meaning hit him with the force of a two-by-four aimed squarely at his head. He pressed his foot to the brake and slowed his truck. "I'm sorry. I didn't mean it like that." He paused, then glanced her way. Her gaze was firmly on the windshield, but telltale moisture at the corners of her eyes said he'd screwed up. Again.

"Grae. You're definitely part of the community. More than you might even think." He crossed the divide between them and placed a hand on her knee. The reassurance was mutual. Whether she understood what changed between them or not, he felt her heartbeat slow and his fell in line to accompany it. A shared deep breath echoed in the cab as they neared the drive to Isaac's apple farm.

"Charlie?"

"Yeah?"

"What did I do so wrong that people want me dead?" Her voice shook again, and the wetness in her eyes spilled out onto her cheeks.

"I don't know, Grae." He shook his head, warring with the anger bubbling beneath the surface of his words. "But I promised to protect you, and I'll do whatever it takes to keep that promise."

He turned off the flashing lights on his truck before heading up Isaac's long driveway. If Roy was behind the murders, he didn't want to draw any unwanted attention to Isaac's place since it was through a tree-line beside Grae's home. He pulled into a spot beside Isaac's old farm truck and cut the engine.

"I need you to trust me, Grae, when I tell you this—" he paused for a moment to gather the courage he needed—"I did something stupid. I didn't think it through, and now it's going to be hard on you. I'm sorry."

The look of confusion crossing her face only made it harder to say the words.

A knock on his window startled them both. Reaching for his firearm at his hip, he whirled in his seat. Familiar silver eyes stared back at him.

"Charles? Is everything all right?"

Charlie relaxed his grip and returned his gun to the holster as Grae threw open the door and raced around the truck. When she fell, sobbing, into Isaac's arms, Charlie's heart broke.

15

*Random Thought # 76 - Coming home crushes all
your worries and shreds your walls. Home is where the
heart is most vulnerable.*

Gracelynn flung her arms around the man she'd
known her entire life. Isaac Strom was the closest thing
she had to a living breathing father, and she needed an
uncomplicated hug in the worst way.

"You know?" Tears ran down her cheeks as sobs
fractured her words.

"How could I not?" The older man replied and
pulled her even deeper into his embrace. "I woke from
a dead sleep when it happened."

"How?"

"Child, your mother and I had a complicated relationship, but it never stopped me from loving her in nearly every way possible." He pressed a chaste kiss to her temple. "I can't believe she's gone."

"I know," she cried. "It's all my fault. Whoever hurt her was looking for me." She pulled back from the embrace and met the kind silver eyes she'd looked to throughout her entire life, when clarity was her aim. Isaac had been the community elder most of her lifetime, and he was beyond kind and fair when it came to her. She assumed it had something to do with the relationship he and her mom shared, but it wasn't until now, looking him in the face, that she knew whatever ran between them had been deeper than she'd ever known.

"Gracelynn, don't you dare go blaming this on yourself," Isaac chided. "Your mother loved you so much. She spent her life trying to protect you from that man and his crazy ideas, but…"

"My father's really behind this?" She hated the acid taste on her tongue when using the word 'father' and standing so close to Isaac. "Mom always said he'd come for me." She shook her head.

"Hush, child. Come inside." He glanced over her shoulder and motioned to Charlie. "And bring your mate."

Her feet froze in place while her heart fumbled to regain its rhythm. "My *what*?" Her voice barely audible, she whirled on Charlie as he unfolded himself from the truck, unable to meet her eyes. "My what?" she repeated, this time loud enough that even the animals in the fields went silent. "What the fuck did you do, Charles Latham?"

"I see," mused Isaac. "I'll go inside while you two sort this out."

"Sort this out? What the hell does that mean?" She turned back to the man in question and aimed a finger at his chest. "Damn it, Charlie! I thought…" She ran the last twenty-four hours through her mind. "He's wrong. It's impossible. You're a Wind, right?"

"Yeah."

One freaking word. That's all he could muster after getting her into this? She shook her head. "We can't be bonded. I'm a half-blood and I'm pretty sure I'm a Water. That's how I ended up down river."

"Sophie was a Wind."

His words sent chills up her spine. "No. She can't have been a Wind if I'm a Water," she argued.

"Well, if you're a Water, then maybe so was your father," Isaac suggested.

"Impossible. His family belonged to a group of Elemental hunters. Why would he hunt a community he belonged to?" She fought to gain control of her racing heart. In all her years, she'd never seen her mom shift into her grounding element. Not even once. She'd always assumed it was because of her half-breed status and her mom's desire to never make her feel left out. But if Charlie was right, there was even less reason for them to be mated. She knew the stories. They had all the hallmarks of a fairy tale with fated partners of the same grounding elements and such. All things she and Charlie weren't. Hell, her mixed blood should ensure she'd never bond in the way of the supernatural community with anyone…ever. Right?

"Have you met Elms' new husband yet?" Charlie asked with a wary look.

"No, why?"

"Simon's a Fire, she's a Wind. It was fated. Things have changed a lot in the last few months around here." He placed a tentative hand on her shoulder. "I'm sorry. If I'd known there was even the slightest possibility..."

"Stop." She interrupted him. "You knew?" She poked his chest with the question, swung on her heel, and stomped in the other direction.

"Not until after it happened."

His defensive tone did little to quash the rush of emotions boiling in her blood stream. "Why didn't you say something? Maybe we could've stopped it." She threw her hands in the air.

"There's no stopping the bonding. It happens. That's it. Plain and simple."

"But isn't that the equivalent of getting married?" Panic clung to the edge of her words.

"In the eyes of the community."

His response was too short. There had to be more to it. "And?"

"And what? We had sex. We bonded, and now we're stuck with each other."

His words stung as if shards of her broken heart had pierced through her skin. So much for bonding being a romantic event that members of the community cherished. She'd witnessed a lot of bonding ceremonies in her childhood, and none included either partner looking less than thrilled at the prospect of spending forever together. Her stomach sank. Of course, it made sense that her bonding would be messed up. Sure. Why not? Her entire life was one big joke for Fate after all.

"Look, we don't have to go through with it," she offered. "I don't want you to be stuck." She turned toward Isaac's home and squared her shoulders. She'd get through this. Whatever the consequences, she'd find a way through. Then she'd leave Harmony and never look back. Ever.

"Grae, wait. It's not that simple. Once a couple bonds, the only way to break it is willfully." He stepped into line beside her as she walked. "And there are residual problems if we do that."

"It's okay. I can willfully decide not to want you, Charlie. And from the sounds of it, you've already decided you can too. So how hard can it be?" She reached the steps leading to the front porch and paused. "I'm sure it happens all the time." She shrugged her shoulder and took the stairs one at a time.

Isaac opened the door for her and ushered her into the house. "You look cold, child."

"Yeah, I had a little mishap. My mom was a Wind?" She tossed the question in as casually as she could, considering all the shit happening in her head.

"Yes, she was. Why?" Isaac studied her as if she was under a microscope.

"Well, I think I might be a Water." She flopped on the couch and hugged a pillow to her chest while avoiding his piercing silver eyes.

"I'm not sure that's possible." The couch sank beside her as he settled his weight. He patted her knee. "I'm sure you've made a mistake. What makes you think you're a Water, Gracelynn?"

She glanced at Charlie as he finally entered the house before she answered. "Well, for one, I've always been drawn to the water. And, for another, when I was in danger, I went to the river and kinda became one with it. I don't know how else to explain it." She hugged the pillow harder and a fresh batch of tears welled in her eyes. "I lost my clothes and shoes. A homeless person found me." The tears escaped. Charlie sat on the edge of the seat closest to where she sat. Refusing to look his way, she swiped at her eyes and ducked her head.

"There, there," Isaac soothed with his gentle pats. "Tell me exactly what happened."

"I don't know. It happened really fast." She wrung the material of the borrowed shirt in her hands and avoided looking at either of the men. "I was in trouble," she started. "And when I had the chance to escape, instead of running for the road or the woods, I went to the water." She paused for a breath and waited. "And then, I just…" She struggled for the best description of how it had felt. "Gave myself over to it. I trusted it to protect me, and it did." She prided herself in her ability to finish strong. "I became one with the river," she clarified. "There's no other way to describe it."

"Was this the first time, Grae?"

Without looking his way, she nodded.

"Do you think you could do it again?" Isaac stood and studied her with renewed intensity.

"I'm not sure." She contemplated the idea of losing herself so fully again.

"Would you be willing to try?"

"Isaac, leave her alone. She's had a rough morning."

"Charles, don't you think it's important to know for sure if your mate is a Water?"

"Does it matter? Look at Elms and Simon. They work just fine."

"Yes, but we don't know what it will mean for that child she's carrying. Precautions should be taken, Charles."

Gracelynn watched as the two men verbally sparred in front of her. She needed a clean set of clothes and a warm shower. And possibly not in that order.

She rose from her spot on the couch, cleared her throat, and when they carried on as if she hadn't uttered a peep, she walked to Charlie's side, stood on her tiptoe, and whispered in his ear. "I need a shower. And clean clothes. Want to help me with either of those, *hubs*?"

His reaction was immediate. "Shower, Isaac?" And his head swiveled as if looking for a shower that might magically appear before his eyes right there in the living room.

"Sure. Down the hall and to the left," the elder answered.

Charlie grabbed her hand in his and pulled her down the hall behind him.

"Is everything okay?"

Isaac's words hit her ears as Charlie dragged her into the bathroom and shut the door seconds after she crossed the threshold. She stood statue still as he moved to the tub and turned the knobs. As if she wasn't there, he bustled about the room, pulling out fresh towels and bottles of this and that.

"Water's warm," he announced after checking it with his hand. "Go ahead and get in."

"Not with you in here." She balked as he removed his firearm and set it on the counter.

"Grae, it's a little late for modesty. We've seen each other naked. I've been inside you. For all intents and purposes, we're married. Take those clothes off."

"No." She lifted her chin and stared him down. She lost herself in the blue of his eyes that reminded her of a cool lake on a warm summer day.

His arms wrapped around her with purpose, but somehow remained gentle, as if he was worried she might break, and he lifted her over his broad shoulder. The space between where she'd stood and the shower wasn't enough for a full-on fight, but she managed to squeal and wiggle before being splattered by the warm stream of water. Charlie held tight, moving them both beneath the spray fully clothed.

"Grae, I need you to trust me. I might not have wanted to be mated to you, but I won't let that stop me from taking care of you. Whatever you need, it'll be my job to provide. Understood?"

"Charlie, stop. It's okay. You and I made a mistake. We'll find a way to fix it." She stopped wiggling and slid a hand through his water-slicked hair. "But it's nice to know you're willing to take this so seriously," she added.

"There's no other way to take it, Grae. People who break the bond suffer for the rest of their lives. Look at your mom. She did it, and she never found happiness."

"What?" She pushed against his shoulder until he released his iron grip. "What about my mom?"

"You can't tell me you don't know." He shook his head and stepped back so the water could warm her.

"Didn't know what?"

"Your mom and Isaac?" He scraped a hand across his jawline scruff. "They were supposedly Fated, but she refused to mate with him because she was already married to your father when they met."

She shivered under his scrutiny. "I had no idea until we arrived today. I mean, I always thought there was something between them, but mom never said anything, and I never saw either of them act on it. I just figured they were good friends." She felt silly as the wet, heavy sweatshirt clung to her body.

"Just take it off, Grae. I'll turn around if you want."

She nodded and he did as promised while she peeled the clothes from her body. She let them fall to the floor of the tub with a thud.

"Can you explain how Mom and Isaac managed to undo their bond?" She asked as the warm spray sluiced down her bare skin.

"Yeah. She said '*No*' and he said, '*Shit,*' and then they lived unhappily-ever-after. Destined to feel the pull to one another, yet physically unable to act upon it." He shrugged out of his wet shirt and met her eyes.

Her fingers itched to trace the path of water traveling down his chest, but she resisted. "So even if they decided to give it a try later, they couldn't?"

"Exactly. A broken bond tears two people apart forever," he answered, meeting her eyes.

"But Mom and Isaac lived normal enough lives," she protested as her mouth dried with the words.

"Oh, really? Did you ever wonder why they had tea together so often?" Charlie toed off his boots, reached for his belt, and began working the buckle. "They needed to be close to maintain some connection. Yet I doubt they ever so much as touched over the years."

"Why not?" Her whispered question had little to do with the subject matter, and everything to do with the skin being revealed as he peeled wet denim off his muscular legs.

"Because the pain it causes is said to be excruciating." He dropped the wet jeans on the bathroom floor and stepped closer. "Kinda like the pain I'm feeling right now."

"But we're not touching." Her voice turned husky as he neared.

"Exactly." His voice dropped low.

Mere inches separated them, breath tangling in the steam. She needed to feel him against her body. Craved the touch of his skin on hers. Maybe Isaac was right. They'd bonded, and this was the reason her blood ran through her veins as if spiked with fire. She hesitated to consider the ramifications of breaking the bond. Imagining never feeling the flex of his muscles beneath her fingertips again made her want to cry out.

As if they reached the decision in unison, her arms wound around his neck at the same time his hands clutched her hips. Water cascaded over them as he lifted her and urged her legs around his waist.

"Damn, Grae. I don't want to hurt you, but I'm not sure I can let you walk away from this." His teeth scraped the tender skin below her ear as he backed her against the tiled wall.

"I don't want to walk away. Not now." She titled her hips, searching for the friction she desired, and sighed. Her brain buzzed like static on the radio. The familiar feel of Charlie's thoughts in her mind was eerily absent as she willed him to take her. She needed him. Now. As if he understood her intrinsic need, he shifted her weight and plunged his hardness into her soft depths with a shudder.

Her nerve endings sparked to life as the noise in her head went blissfully silent. Nothing resonated beyond the feel of Charlie deep within, anchoring them together. His tongue found the hollow of her collarbone— tasting, teasing, tempting her senses. Hands clung with every ounce of strength to hold her fast as her back slid against the tile. Teeth grazed her ear with the perfect amount of pressure to send her eyes into the back of her head. Bliss. Utterly surrounded by the steam and water and Charlie. Gracelynn's life made sense, even if only for this moment in time. She arched her back, wordlessly inviting him to explore her, while giving her the added friction she craved at their juncture.

He nipped and licked his way across every available inch of her skin, sending her straddling the edge of bliss before his mouth returned to hers. Home again, she opened herself under the weight of his stare.

His blue eyes—deeper than the ocean, yet lighter than the sky—twinkled. "You, Grae, might be the best mistake I've ever made."

She smiled against his lips and gave herself over to the pressure building between them. Moments later, she shattered. Unable to hold onto his broad shoulders any longer, she succumbed to the spray of the water cascading over her skin. Caressing each droplet with a piece of her soul, she lost the battle and surrendered, dripping down this man she had longed for over the years, craved now with a fierce hunger, and was supernaturally bonded to forever. Her consciousness was aware, yet disjointed, as if she existed in a million tiny little bits all clamoring to touch the man inside her at once.

Her release came quaking from the depths of her being as Charlie shook with his own. His hands grabbed for purchase, but seemingly ran through her. She existed everywhere and nowhere, all in the same instant.

Bliss.

16

Random Thought # 93 - That girl knows how to take the Wind out of a guy's sails.

Grae disappeared in a splash of water, and Charlie froze. Shit. He'd screwed up again. Not only had he bonded with a Water, but he'd fucked her in her element. He needed to get a grip, before he condemned them both to a lifetime of pain and despair. Before he could contemplate it further, a door banged against the wall of the bathroom.

"Charlie? You in here?"

"Dude! You gotta knock," he growled as Colin spoke. He turned off the spray and wondered if he should plug the drain for Grae. *What are you supposed to do after fucking a Water into her Elemental form?*

"Where's Gracie? That officer tried to take her, but I think she got away."

Charlie opened the curtain and stepped out. "She's okay. Turns out she's more like us than we thought."

"What?" Colin passed him a towel and stepped from the room. "How so?" He called from around the corner of the doorway.

Charlie attempted to dry his body, but a fine layer of moisture clung to him like a second skin, putting a smile on his face. *Shit, that is sexy.* He shook his thoughts away and focused on the task at hand. "She's a Water," he answered. "Lost her clothes in the river, but was able to escape."

Laughter was Colin's response.

"Yeah, it was pretty amusing," Charlie agreed, but as the words left his mouth, the droplets of water on his skin vibrated, and for the first time since they'd entered the shower, he could feel the mental brush of her mind against his. And his woman wasn't happy. The shimmering on his skin continued until he was dry and Grae stood whole beside him, hand on her hip, and an irritated look on her face.

"Charlie Latham, how dare you?"

All she lacked was the stomping foot of a full-out tantrum.

"I was just teasing. So... this happen often?" He made a raining gesture with his hands and waited as her face shifted to a light blush. "I see," he mused. "Only for me, huh?"

Her fist connected with his arm before he saw it coming. Even when she was mad, she was sexy as hell.

"Are you going to hand me a towel or just stand there gawking?"

"Can I vote for the gawking?" Colin called from the hallway.

Another fist landed benign against Charlie's arm. With a smile, he passed the annoyed woman a towel. "I'm going to see if I can get into your mom's place and get you something to wear," he offered, knowing full-well he could lose his badge for this.

"My suitcase is in my bedroom and mostly still packed," she replied as she toweled her long hair, her breasts bouncing with her movement. "Unless one of the dicks went through it."

"I'm sure it's fine." Staring was a bad idea, but he couldn't help himself. She was long and lean, but had enough curves to make his mouth water. Little did she know, but those damn curves should come with a warning where he was concerned. From the first time he noticed she'd gotten them back in high school, he'd itched to get his hands on them.

"What do we do next? I can't go into the station if one of the cops there is trying to kill me, right?"

Her words chilled him. What *should* he do with her? If he didn't take her in, he risked losing his badge. But if he did, he risked losing his mate. *Aww, hell.* "Let me call in and see what the captain has to say. See if he knows you've gone missing, and I'll take it from there. In the meantime, you stay here with Isaac and Colin. No leaving the house. Understand?"

"Yeah. I'll stay put."

Satisfied, Charlie hung his towel on a hook behind the door and joined Colin in the hallway. "You okay to stick around and keep an eye on her?"

"Sure thing. What's your plan, exactly?"

"Fly home, Get some fresh clothes, and See if anyone is hanging around still. Then I'll come back and call into the precinct. See what's going on."

"All right. What do you want me to do if someone comes here looking for her?" His friend's cheeks turned red as he jerked his eyes back to Charlie, scrubbed at the top of his head, and did his best to avoid looking toward the bathroom.

Charlie turned in time to catch Grae's naked reflection in the mirror. "How about you go ask Isaac for something she can wear until I can get her stuff, then do whatever it takes to keep her safe? Right now, you're the only person I can trust."

"What about Dec? I'll bet he and Simon would be willing to do some digging to see who's dirty on the force."

It wasn't a bad idea, but Charlie hated asking for favors. "Maybe." His noncommittal answer bounced back at him in Grae's voice inside his head.

"Maybe? You want to catch these assholes or what? If someone can help, ask them, you stubborn ox."

Life with her was going to be interesting.

~•~

Shifting into his Elemental form before he left Isaac's farm was as commonplace as chewing his food. "Second nature" came to mind when describing it to Elementals of other groundings.

He glided along on the currents as his thoughts wandered. Images of years long ago flashed across his thoughts.

Grae in the denim romper painting that crazy mailbox with her mom one summer, hair all braided, paint smeared on her cheek. Grae in a dress on the arm of some boy he had to bite his lip to keep from telling to stop touching her in high school at a semi-formal. Grae in the woods, playing a dangerous game of spin the bottle as a campfire crackled behind her. The feel of her warm lips under his as the bottle he'd spun pointed in her direction. The look in her eyes as he crawled over the ground to meet her, and the way she trembled ever so slightly as their breath tickled each other's faces. The taste of cinnamon and sweetness of her mouth as his tongue darted between her parted lips. The sigh he still heard in his dreams some nights after they'd parted ways. The sad tilt of her head when he refused to meet her eyes again that evening.

To this day, he didn't forgive himself for kissing her that night. He should've given her a simple peck on the cheek and moved on. But no, he'd gone and kissed her until he'd been senseless. The kind of kiss worthy of curling his toes and making his shorts uncomfortable for longer than he cared to admit.

And now he'd be kissing her for the rest of his life.

The thought put an abrupt halt on everything in his mind. Gracelynn George was essentially his wife. The part of his brain responsible for continuing his path faltered, and he almost dropped his Elemental nature and plummeted to the ground.

Shit.

Images of her opening her legs for him assaulted his better judgment. The sweet taste of her nectar on his lips begged him to turn around and go back to her. *Now.* Her long, silky hair wrapped around his hand as he plunged into her as she bent over the tailgate of his truck.

Shit. Shit. Shit.

The ache in his heart grew, and the yearning to claim her again clawed at his insides, demanding to be satisfied. The pain. Physical pain lanced through his heart, taking the wind out of his sails, halting his movement. *Shit.* He needed to go back for her. How dumb was he to leave her alone? With other men. *Shit.*

Knowing their bond now lay cemented between them was no comfort to him. Rather, he wanted to race back to Isaac's and demand she go with him. The idea of letting her out of his sight drove him wild. Untethered and panic-stricken, it occurred to him he was closer to his home than Isaac's. Home offered what he needed. He had a purpose. Keeping her safe. And to do that, he needed clothes. Home it was.

Pushing against the pain pulling him back, he seeped beneath the back door and flowed into his house. Initial inspection showed no signs of struggle or sense of wrongdoing. All locked up nice and tight as if no one had been there.

He ebbed into his bedroom and shifted back into his human form. Without waiting, he pulled socks, a tee, and jeans from the drawers and slid into them. Boots followed. If he moved quickly, he could whip up a cup of Sophia's magic potion and get back before Grae began suffering the effects of his absence. While in his closet looking for his favorite blue flannel, the creak of floorboards dumped adrenaline into his bloodstream.

Stepping farther into the closet, he reached for the small safe on the top shelf. Keying in the code wasn't a silent endeavor, but once done, he'd be armed. He held his breath and listened with his mind.

"Come on out, Latham. I know you're here. And you're one of *them*." Elroy's voice echoed in the small house.

Fingers on the keypad, Charlie punched in the code and withdrew his loaded Glock 26. It was small in his hands, but it had eleven bullets ready to aim in Roy's direction.

The face-off felt like something out of the movies. Each stepping into the other's view at precisely the same moment, guns raised and ready to shoot. The silent echo of heartbeats thundered around them as each man studied the other.

"How did you hide it all these years?"

"Hide what?"

"What you are," Elroy spat. "There wasn't any indication you were anything but human. But that woman comes back to town, and now it's obvious."

"I don't know what you're talking about, Roy." Charlie only half-listened to the other man's spoken words as he concentrated on the flash of thoughts humming in Elroy's brain. "Gracelynn George is an old friend and a member of this community."

"Charlie, we've known each other too long for this bullshit. She and her mother are freaks. You know it, and I know it."

"I don't agree with you, man. All I see is you in my house uninvited, with a gun in my face. If there's anyone who's looking like a freak right now, it's you." Charlie took the calculated risk and lowered his aim a smidge. "What makes you think they have something to hide? Sophie took care of the people of this town for years. Helping deliver babies, working with the sick, helping the elderly. She was practically the best damn doctor who wasn't really a doctor around. Definitely better than those frauds who have medical degrees at the hospital two towns over. Hell, more people in Harmony were on her patient list than drove the number who bothered to drive the thirty minutes to see a real M.D. How can someone like that be anything other than good for the town?"

"She wasn't using skill to help those people. She used magic." Roy's tone dropped from anger to conspiratorial sharing. "Those women aren't human."

"You realize you sound delusional right now?" Charlie accused, ready for what he knew would come next.

"Shut the fuck up, Latham. You're one of them," Roy exploded, and his arm jerked upward as he pressed his finger against the trigger.

Charlie ducked, and the round landed in the wall above his head. He used his low stance and threw his weight into the man, knocking him to the ground. They fought for control of Roy's gun for only the briefest of moments before Charlie managed to subdue him.

"Stop struggling, Roy. You've lost your mind. Gone off the deep end. There isn't such a thing as..." He tried to jog his memory for what Roy had called the women. Coming up blank, he supplied, "Witches."

Roy spat in his face and struggled against his hold. "Witches would be a picnic compared to what these things are. They're in the same league as vampires and werewolves," he cried. "You know I'm telling the truth. You're one of them too."

"Roy, I think you've lost your freaking mind. I'm the same person I've always been," Charlie insisted.

"You mean the same guy who solved cases with no evidence. Dragged confessions out of people who supposedly refused to speak. I've see the signs over the years, but I didn't recognize them for what they were. I just thought you were a good cop."

The slight stung. Charlie *was* a damn good cop. He just had an advantage the others didn't. Sure, it was a boost, but it didn't diminish the work he'd done.

Before he could begin to formulate a rebuttal, the invisible chord tying Grae to him, snapped. His world went to pitch, and his soul screamed. What the fuck had she done?

17

Random Thought # 227 - Living a lie isn't living. It's only lying.

Gracelynn paced Isaac's house like a caged animal. He'd found an old pair of pajama pants that seemed to fit all right and a sweatshirt that reminded her of her mom for her to wear. No longer naked, she needed to burn off some of the energy coursing through her veins. Ever since Charlie left, she'd fought a restlessness she couldn't explain. With each lap of the living room, the desire to go find him grew more overwhelming.

"Here, drink this," Isaac advised and placed a warm mug in her hands.

"What is it?" She sniffed at the contents and wrinkled her nose as licorice assaulted her senses. "Ew, is this Mom's tea? Her homemade one?" She handed the mug back, her heart heavy.

"It is." Isaac nodded and pushed the cup back into her hands. "Trust me when I tell you to drink this, child. Your mother was brilliant at her life's work, and this is one thing she created that no one even knows exists."

"But it tastes awful," she argued, as she held the steaming concoction at arm's length. "I tried it as a kid once."

"Of course it tasted awful then. You weren't yet mated. Try it now," he insisted before turning back to the kitchen and returning with a matching mug for himself.

With a tentative sip, the first splash of the tea on her tongue tasted like twilight, light with a dark undertone, mysterious and exciting. She swallowed the sip and eagerly drank the mug dry. "She must've improved the recipe."

"Recipe is the same."

She watched as he gently sipped his tea, closing his eyes as if savoring the flavor. After a beat, he met her gaze and continued.

"It's meant to settle a restless heart; one searching for its lost mate," he explained and set his cup on the coffee table. "Your mom and I—"—

"I know," she interrupted. "Fated mates who didn't work out."

"Not exactly." The elder sat on the couch and patted the cushion beside him. "I loved your mother with my whole heart. The moment I laid eyes on her, I knew. She was to be my mate, and I was to be hers. It took a month of seeing her around town for me to gather the courage to speak to her. She was radiant, glowing even. I ignored the rumors of a husband and child on the way, because I knew in the deepest space in my soul, there wasn't anyone besides her for me.

"One day, I was in the fields picking and saw a truck drive up next door. Out stepped a man and woman. I watched as they walked to the front door and met the Realtor. The two men went inside, but the woman... She stopped, as if she knew I watched her from afar, and turned my way. Your mother didn't follow the men. No. She walked around to the back of the house, through the trees, and crossed the little stream that separates the properties. Instead of joining me in the orchards, she sat on a bench overlooking the area that's now my garden. The slump of her shoulders drew me to her as fast as my legs could carry me." Isaac stopped his story and sipped his tea, a wistful look on his face.

"What happened?" Waiting had never been Grace-lynn's strong suit, and this intimate glimpse into her mother's past intrigued her. She settled on the couch beside Isaac and ran her finger around the edge of her mug while she waited for him to continue.

"It wasn't about what happened so much as it was about why she was crying," he answered. "Her sadness nearly destroyed me, and we hadn't even yet spoken," he explained before taking a long sip and returning his drink to the table. "I will never forget the first words she spoke to me. 'I'm sorry, Mate, my heart belongs to another.' I remember feeling as if the very heart she spoke of was being ripped from her chest as abruptly as it was being forced from my own."

Gracelynn watched as he absently rubbed a hand over the invisible wound on his chest. "How could she know? You said you'd never talked. Never kissed or..." She let the rest of her thought die off. "What I mean is, Charlie and I kissed before, and nothing happened with the bond until we..." Wow, nothing she tried to say came out right. "I mean," she tried again after a long, deep breath.

"I know what you mean, Gracelynn." Isaac chuckled. "The first time you kissed Charles, you were young, correct?"

"Yes. It was back when I was sixteen." She blushed as the memory of the spin the bottle kiss bubbled to the surface. Seconds later, she got a mental replay of the kiss in his car the time he'd been home on Spring Break and found her after the prom. How had she let that moment slip her mind?

"Ah... Charles was about eighteen at the time, wasn't he?"

The question caught her off guard and pulled her back to the present. She thought about that very first kiss. A summer night. Sure enough, it was the end of the summer, before he went off to college. "I think so," she agreed, nodding.

"Interesting." Isaac's fingers danced on his knee while he stared off into the distance.

"What does his age have to do with anything?"

"Charles has been drinking this tea for many years. I've seen him select it at your mother's, and he's requested it here. The bond you two created began long ago, Gracelynn, whether you knew it or not." He scratched his chin and eyed her closely. "When you and Charlie sealed your bond, who initiated it, if I might ask?"

"I did." The admission sent a blush rushing to her face as flames licked through her bloodstream. "Charlie tried very hard to be a gentleman." Why she was defending him, she wasn't sure, but it felt right.

"Oh, I'm certain he was." Isaac nodded. "Charles bonded with you before you were ready for the bond. Knowing your mother as I did, I bet she saw him for some concentration issues once he left for college. I'd even wager she suspected he'd begun to bond with an underage Elemental and prescribed him this tea."

"Why? How?" So many questions raced through her mind. She was on her feet, pacing, before her head could make sense of all the thoughts running through it. "Oh my God, was that why he kissed me in the bar last night?" She paused her pacing and whirled on Isaac.

"Possibly. I'm sure that young man has been dreaming of kissing you for the last ten years."

"No." The word consisted less of actual sounds and more of air hissing from between her teeth. "It's not possible." She shook her head, refusing to believe his words.

A knowing smile accompanied his meaning-laden, "Ah."

"No, no, no. That can't be right. I wasn't an Elemental then."

"You've always been an Elemental, Gracelynn, despite your insistence to the contrary. How long have you been dreaming of Charles?"

The abrupt shift in the conversation made her want to fall to the ground, wailing. He knew. The man who'd so often been there throughout her life knew her secret.

"I can't say," she rebuked.

"Monthly? Weekly?"

"Isaac," she warned.

"I see," he countered. "That often, huh?"

Before she could come up with anything that would get him off his line of questioning, Colin came in through the front door. "No sign of him yet. I really thought he'd be back here by now."

Gracelynn's heart jumped to double time in her chest as she searched the room for a clock. It had felt like Charlie'd been gone forever, but the newly-formed bond was explanation enough for that. If Colin was concerned, that was something else entirely.

"Where did he say he was going?" she asked.

"Home. Clothes first, then something about calling in to see if anyone reported you missing, I think."

"Can you drive his truck?"

"Gracelynn, we all know Charles wanted you to stay here," Isaac reminded her.

She ignored him and turned a piercing gaze on Colin.

"Yup, but I'm pretty sure he wouldn't want me to," Colin hedged.

"We need to go find him. If he was only going home for a change of clothes, he should've been back by now. So you can either drive his truck, or you can give me directions and I'll drive." She left the men alone in the living room to search for Charlie's keys. Lucky on the first try, she found them tucked inside the wet pocket of his jeans. Then she grabbed the piles of wet clothes from the floor and stuffed them into the tub until later. She'd worry about them once Charlie was here. As she passed the sink, she made a quick decision and grabbed the gun he'd left behind. A sense of dread settled in her gut.

"You're a Wind, right?" she asked Colin as she rounded the corner into the main living space.

"Yeah?"

"Good. Breeze on over to my mom's, will ya? I need a change of clothes and some shoes. As long as no one's there, you can bring the stuff to me."

"Ugh, I'm not supposed to leave you alone." Panic crept into Colin's eyes.

"Look, you can either help me get the stuff, or I'll go over there myself. Worst case, there are officers there and they take me in." She shrugged. When it came to losing, she didn't have much left to hold on to beyond her dignity, and that hung from a very thin thread.

"How about if I call Charlie, and check when he'll be back?" Colin asked as she turned away and headed into the kitchen.

For her entire life, she remembered Isaac kept his work boots just outside the back door, and if all went according to plan, she'd be wearing them in under a minute. *Score.* She let the back screen door bang shut behind her as she stuffed her feet into the too big boots.

"Gracie, stop," Colin called as she made her way down the back steps.

She ignored his pleas and tucked Charlie's gun in the waistband of the sleep pants. She was a woman on a mission. Step one, figure out which key on the ring was for the truck. The second key worked as hoped, so she slid into the cab and cranked over the engine. Before she could get the seat adjusted, Colin climbed in shotgun.

"What do you think you're doing? Have you lost your mind? Charlie will kick my ass if anything happens to you."

"Get out." She fumbled with the electronic bar on the side of the seat to move it far enough that she could reach the pedals.

"No. I told Charlie I'd keep an eye on you. A promise is a promise." He reached over the space between their seats and removed the key from the ignition. "And I'll tell you something else, Charlie loves this truck. It's probably the only thing in the world he actually loves. And if he knew I was letting you drive it, he'd be pissed. So switch."

"I can handle the truck." She wanted to turn her lip out and convince the human fridge beside her that she was more than capable of driving the vehicle, but reading his brain waves, she knew it would be a futile argument. "All right," she huffed, and hopped down from the cab.

Colin met her halfway as they crossed paths to the opposite doors like a darn Chinese fire drill. He stopped only inches from her and blocked her way with his broad chest.

"I know you're stressed out, but I need you to calm down and let me think, okay? It's important I keep my word to Charlie, but I understand where you're coming from. So cut me a little slack, all right?" His silver eyes held the weight of a weary warrior.

"It's a deal." She offered him her hand, hoping he would read the sincerity behind the gesture. During their brief stand-off, she'd witnessed enough of his personal thoughts to know it wasn't fair to put him in the situation he was in. Charlie never should've asked him to watch after her. He'd seen too much already in his short life, and there were pockets of darkness in his head even she couldn't access. Colin was a wounded bird if ever she'd seen one.

When he finally put his hand in hers to shake, images rushed at her with the force of a tornado let loose. She saw strange things. A woman, bloodied and wounded, lying on the ground. She wasn't fully human, if the wings and tail were any indicators, but Gracelynn felt the love in Colin's heart when she looked at her. He was smitten. Completely and utterly lost to her. The next scene that flashed before her was of Colin sitting at a table with a bunch of people she didn't recognize. He and a woman who looked a lot like the fallen demon from the first memory were toasting something. The word 'forget' wafted through her brain, and her heart sank. Poor guy. His true love wasn't a mate the community would approve of. Knowing that, he'd made the ultimate sacrifice.

She let go of his hand and studied him closely. "Hey, can I ask you a personal question?" She kicked the toe of Isaac's boot against the gravel drive.

"Sure. Shoot."

"Do you hurt, ever?"

"What do you mean?"

The look on his face screamed he thought she was nuts, but she ignored it. "I mean, what would you do if your mate wasn't someone the community would approve of? How would you feel about it?"

"I don't know," he replied slowly. "I guess I don't think about the idea of finding my mate all that often." He shrugged his shoulders. "Why?"

"I see things in my head sometimes. And it's not always stuff people want me to see," she started. "But I saw something in you that made me wonder…"

"Wonder about my mate? I haven't met her yet," he insisted.

"I think you did, though. And I think you decided to break the bond because she wasn't part of the Elemental Community." As his face crumbled, she regretted even saying a single word. "Colin, I'm sorry. I didn't mean anything by it. I was just thinking if you had found a way to get around the bonding process, maybe you could help Charlie too. I know he doesn't want to be stuck with me. Based on what Isaac said, he's worked really hard for a long time to ensure he doesn't have to consider the possibility of being stuck to me forever. That's all. Really. I didn't mean anything by it."

"It's okay, Gracie. But I think you're mistaken. If I'd met my mate, I'd remember." He stepped around her and moved toward the driver's side of the truck.

"But you wouldn't remember if you took a potion."

"Why would I take a potion to forget meeting my mate?" Colin stopped short, his spine went iron rod straight, and his shoulders squared.

"The word 'forget' triggered something, didn't it?" She raced to his side and placed her hands on his biceps. "I can help you find her," she gushed, needing to make it right. "I saw her in your memory. She was beautiful. Long dark hair, crystalline blue eyes, wings..."

"Stop! I don't want to know. If I took a Forget potion, there must've been a darn good reason."

"But this is your mate. Don't you want to make sure she's okay? I mean, if you broke the bond, what if she's suffering?"

"Let it go, Gracie." His tone rang of warning.

"How about I make you a deal? I'll help you find her if you can help me figure out a way to save Charlie from a future of heartache. Sound fair?"

"No. It doesn't sound fair, Gracie. I don't want to meddle in Charlie's affairs. I don't want to know what you saw. And I sure don't want you digging around in my head anymore. Understand?"

His voice was so deep and low it shook her to her core. Unsure how to proceed, she just nodded and moved around to the passenger side. So much for a partner in crime in Colin. With her luck, she'd just made a new enemy.

∼◡◠

Gracelynn's house was deserted when they arrived. Perfect. Her mom kept a spare key hidden under a stepping stone in the back walkway, right near a piece of half buried rose quartz shaped like a heart. Isaac's words crashed around her like a tidal wave. Her mother had spent her whole life trying to repair her broken mating. And now, here she was, about to do the same thing for Charlie's sake.

She unwrapped the key from its hiding spot beneath the stone and unlocked the rear door. "Will you stand watch? I'll only be a minute or two."

"Yeah. Be quick." Colin's answer stung.

She hurried her way through her childhood home in record time, collecting her suitcase and anything else that made sense in the moment. On her way back through the house, she stopped and considered her mom's apothecary. Maybe she could find the solution to the bond issue in there. Weighing the pros and cons took only a second. Charlie had suffered enough because of her. If her mom had a way to dissolve the bond without consequence, she was going to find it.

She opened the back door and set the suitcase on the top step. "Hey, can you put this is the truck? I need to look for something in my mom's clinic. I'll be right out."

"'Kay."

She ignored Colin's grumpy one-word answer and darted back in the house. Her mom was meticulous about how her clinic was arranged, but if she had something as important as the cure for the bonding process side effects, she wouldn't likely keep it out and on display with all her other tinctures and cures. Would she?

Uncertain, Gracelynn went first to the huge antique apothecary cabinet that took up the majority of the wall behind the makeshift counter. Pawing through the vials and baggies turned up nothing helpful. She dropped to her knees behind the counter and began opening little drawers. Nothing screamed 'bonding cure,' but one drawer held the familiar scent of the licorice tea. Small tins of loose leaf ingredients were stacked neatly unlabeled. Behind them sat small vials with *Forget* scrawled on the labels. And behind them, even smaller vials with *Fade* written in her mom's script.

The pale red liquid caught her eye and sucked her in. Fade? She gave another glance to the vials labeled Forget and considered her options.

"Come on, Gracie. Charlie's gonna be pissed if he gets back to Isaac's and both you and his truck are missing."

Colin took up the whole doorway leading from the kitchen into her mom's healing arts studio, and the look on his face was nothing less than annoyed.

"I think I found what I'm looking for," she quipped. "Do you know anything about the *Forget* potion?"

"Yeah, and it's probably a good idea if you stay far away from it," he warned. "Elms' husband took it and almost destroyed them. The side effects can be as un-predictable as the efficacy." He loomed over her shoulder, his breath warm on her neck.

"How so?" She lifted one of the small vials from the drawer and gave it a closer inspection.

"Because I took it once and I remember everything. Shit didn't work." Colin grabbed the vial from her hand and put it back in the drawer with a hard clink.

"Careful!"

"You're the one who needs to be careful. This stuff isn't all it's cracked up to be, Gracie. I know your mom was pretty smart and all, but she wasn't perfect. And neither is this concoction." He stood to his full height and offered her his hand. "Let's go. Charlie will worry."

She gave a reluctant nod of agreement. "Go start the truck, I'm right behind you." As soon as Colin moved toward the door, she snatched three vials of *Fade*. One she opened and drank immediately before pocketing the remaining tubes. Gracelynn gave the room one long, last look. Even on a day like today, when the world felt emptier, this room felt full of life. Memories of her mom remained tucked in every small detail—every remedy carefully labeled with her delicate script, every freaking ray of sunshine. Whatever resolve had kept Gracelynn focused and functioning dissolved with the ferocity of a freight train, and she fell to the floor in a heap of tears.

First running into Charlie and bonding with him, then losing her mom, and now knowing her life expectancy was shorter than expected. If all worked according to plan...

The click of the center's main door behind her only barely registered in her brain, until the accompanying brain waves dictated danger.

"You look just like her."

The voice held no malice, but its depth conjured images of darkness with every syllable. Gracelynn scrambled to her feet and whirled on the stranger. "I'm sorry, we're closed." She latched on to every fleeting thought she could grasp floating through the man's mind, but most were truncated and abbreviated in disjointed ways, making not a lick of sense.

"I know," he soothed. "I heard the healer had an accident."

His words chilled her. She opened her mind to find Colin's, to see if he was still outside, but she couldn't feel him. Panic sent her heart into double time, and her hands slicked with sweat. "More than an accident," she countered. "In fact, I think the detectives should be back here any moment." She glanced in the direction of a clock hanging on the wall.

"I don't think so," he challenged. "That ring you wear"—he pointed at her finger—"belonged to my mother. Did she tell you that?"

Gracelynn fingered the sapphire she'd worn since her thirteenth birthday. "No." Her honesty surprised her.

"I'm not surprised." He nodded. "I assume she didn't tell you the women in our family tend to have a particular draw to water, did she?"

"What do you mean?"

"Come on. Don't lie to me about it." He cracked his knuckles against his thigh and smirked. "I should've known that you'd be like my mother. Her kind was always fluid with things like the truth," he accused as he stepped farther into the small waiting area.

"I'm not sure what you're trying to say." She cocked her head to the side and stepped behind the counter, willing the separation it provided to act as a deterrent.

"You know, the last time I laid eyes on you was nearly twenty-six years ago," he mused. "You had this great head of soft dark hair, just like Sophie's, and these gold rimmed eyes. They shone like starlight." He stepped closer and leaned on the counter. "Your mother was so pleased."

"How do you know my mom?" His answer floated through her head before the words left his lips.

"I'm your father."

18

*Random thought # 99 - When things appear to be
at their worst, double down and roll with it.*

Unable to manage the man flailing beneath him,
and the emptiness in his chest, Charlie's fists flew into
action. The first landed front and center in Elroy's
smug face. The second one snapped against Roy's jaw.
His former partner went silent and stopped fighting.
The noise in Charlie's head died away with Roy's consciousness. Rising to his feet, he realized he'd just
made a bad situation worse. A set of cuffs dangled
from Roy's belt. Charlie, freed them, then fastened
them around Roy's wrists. Calling this in was the right

thing to do. He knew it was, but a very big part of him wanted to drag Roy out into the woods and let the bears that roamed these parts have him.

He paced the room and tried to make sense of all he'd learned. Roy had some ideas about the Elemental Community, but he hadn't said anything concrete. Maybe it was just a hunch. And if so, it shouldn't be hard to discredit him and ensure Grae's safety.

Roy's phone began ringing in the clip on his belt, and the captain's number illuminated on the screen. Reflex had Charlie reaching for the device before he thought it through.

"Latham here," he answered.

"Latham? I thought I dialed Traver."

"You did, sir. He's just a bit..." Charlie searched for an appropriate word to describe the unconscious man. "Indisposed at the moment."

"Is everything okay out there? I heard there were reports of another dump site, but never got a call from Traver on the status of it." Captain Franklin's voice crackled over the connection. "Do we have another victim or not?"

"No, Captain. I went out there myself this morning and didn't find anything."

"Damn. I thought we might be getting closer to catching whoever is doing this."

Charlie could hear someone talking to the captain in the background.

"No, not another dump site; must've been a false alarm. Yeah, call them in and let's get moving back to the George place. If this sicko is still out there, we need to find anything we can to catch him before another woman winds up dead. Yeah. Okay." The captain switched his attention back to Charlie. "Finally, Latham, is the George woman still with you?"

"No sir, there was an incident here at the house so I took her somewhere safe."

"What kind of incident?" Franklin's voice dropped an octave. "Is she all right? That poor woman has already been through enough."

"Sir?" Confusion nipped at the nape of his neck and sent his hackles rising.

"Gracelynn George," he stated. "I knew her back in college. A sweet girl who always seemed a little lost. Out of place, maybe."

"I didn't know you had a connection to the family," Charlie hedged.

"No, nothing like that. We were friendly. Shared a class or two and belonged to the same study group. She talked about this town like it was full of poison. I remember thinking, when I was offered the job here, that maybe one day I could help make it safe enough she'd want to come home."

The wistful tone in his commander's voice sent Charlie's blood boiling. How dare the captain think he should be the one to protect Grae and make her feel safe and secure? That was his job. She was his. Charlie's squeezed his eyes closed against the assault of runaway jealousy and took a deep breath before continuing. "I'm sure she'd appreciate a safe place to come home to, sir but right now, it's more important to find the person responsible for all this." He toed at Roy's leg and watched for the slightest movement. Nothing.

"Agreed. What happened this morning?"

"Well, someone tried to break into my place while I was at the crime scene. I had a friend here looking after her, and she was able to get away."

"Shit. Do you have a description of the guy?"

"I can do you one better, Captain. It's Traver. He broke in and tried to assault her based on what I've been told. She's safe now, and I have him ready to be brought in."

"Traver? Shit. Are you sure?"

"Sure as he's cuffed here on my bedroom floor, sir."

"I mean, you're sure he attacked her?"

Charlie could hear the disbelief in Franklin's voice and it irked him. "I'm as sure as I can be," he reiterated.

"Damn. I thought he could handle it."

"Handle what?"

"Something came down from way above my head. A special task force. Supposedly, there've been some strange reports coming in from all over the state with people crying supernatural situations. The powers that be assigned each precinct a manpower count for the task force. Being ours is small, we only needed one. Traver's worked with the best for years and I thought he could handle it. I mean, I'm sure it was nothing, but you don't question the powers that be."

Charlie swallowed against the lump that formed in his throat. Humans investigating supernaturals? And he hadn't even known. So much for being the great protector of the Elemental Community. On the floor, Roy began to groan.

"So has this task force found anything concrete? Because Roy was spouting some pretty wild nonsense." His pulse beat hard in the hand holding the phone too tight.

"Not that I'm aware. I should've put you on it, but it's common knowledge you're looking to make a change soon. Bring Traver in, Latham. We'll get to the bottom of this." The line went dead with Franklin's order.

Shit. He slid the phone into his pocket and swore once more for good measure. He'd left his truck at

Isaac's with his cell. If that wasn't enough to keep him from doing his job, the emptiness growing in his chest might.

"Let me up, Latham," Roy ordered with a groan.

"Look, man. I don't know what's gotten into you, but I think you've lost it. Gracelynn isn't some sort of supernatural monsters, and neither was her mom. They're people, Roy. I don't know what you got mixed up in, but you can't go around hunting and killing people."

"Killing people? What the hell are you talking about?" Roy scrambled to a sitting position and struggled against the cuffs. "I didn't kill anyone. I was investigating them."

"Grae told me you were here to hurt her earlier," Charlie accused, showing his hand. "And you all but accused me of being one of whatever you think she is."

"I wasn't here to hurt her. I had orders to bring her in for testing."

"Testing?"

"Yeah. Something popped in the DNA analysis of her mother." A smug look washed across Roy's face. "And I bet anything it would pop, not only in her daughter's, but also yours."

"DNA doesn't come back that fast. You and I both know it," Charlie shook his head and stared down the man he'd trusted to have his six for the last few years. How had he missed the changes?

"When you have a designated team of super scientists at your disposal, yes it does."

"So you weren't planning to hurt Grae?"

"Hell no. I'm not a monster, Latham. You know me. But I can't let monsters like her continue to go running around with the public. It's not safe."

Charlie paced the room and took his time choosing his next words. "You mean, monsters like us, don't you?" He eyed Roy and debated his decision.

"Yes."

Done. "I can't let you loose to hurt anyone again, Roy." He stood tall and squared his shoulders. "We had a good thing, but you can't go through this world accusing people of stuff like this."

From outside, the sound of a car door met his ears, and Colin's panicked brainwaves coursed through his head as if intentionally aimed his way. "Stay put, Roy," he warned with a point of his finger as he left the man on the floor and hurried to the front door.

"Where is she?" he snapped before Colin even made it up to the porch.

"How the hell should I know. One minute she was in Sophie's studio, and the next I saw taillights speeding away up the drive and she's gone."

"Why didn't you follow her?" Charlie jumped down from the porch and raced toward Colin.

"I tried, but they got a pretty impressive head start. Didn't wanna flip your truck coming down the mountain."

"Did you see who she was with?"

"No. I didn't even see the car arrive. I shouldn't've left her alone, man. I'm sorry."

Colin's sincerity ebbed with every word he spoke and stained Charlie's soul. "It wasn't your fault. But I do need another favor."

"Anything."

"Can you call Dec and ask him and Simon to do some research on a NJPD task force? Supposedly pretty hush-hush and looking for proof of supernaturals."

"Okay, man. I'll get right on it."

"I also need you to stay here and keep an eye on Elroy. Turns out, he's part of the group, and they might be involved in Grae's disappearance. I can't let him slink away until I know where she is, and if she's safe."

Colin nodded his head. "Whatever you need." He started walking toward the house, then stopped and turned. "So can I mess with him a little?"

The twinkle in his friend's eyes brought a smile to Charlie's lips. "Why not? Just be careful." He rounded the truck and slid into the driver's seat. He needed to get to the bottom of this task force, and the best place to do that was headquarters. He shifted the Dodge into reverse and backed out the drive. Even if the secret task force wasn't behind Grae's disappearance, maybe they'd stumbled on something that would lead him to the answers he needed.

When he crossed the border into the next county, it occurred to him he no longer sensed the bond. Somehow, he felt untethered. Lost. For as long as he could remember, she'd been a constant in his life. The girl who looked so sad as a child at their first playdate. The girl whose eyes lit like fireworks when he offered her his most prized stuffed animal to play with. The girl he'd watched from afar for years, knowing he'd never have her for his own.

Now, she *was* his. And all the things he expected to feel were absent. Yet loneliness didn't plague him, instead, determination set in. He'd find her and reclaim whatever they might've lost. He'd prove to her they belonged together. His reservations hadn't been about her, but about his sense of self-preservation.

His cell chimed from the cup holder. He must've left it there earlier and forgotten about it. He slowed and read the display. Declan. He immediately pressed the button to connect the call.

"That was fast," Declan answered. "Were you able to get the name of the task force?"

"No, but my old partner's a part of it. Try adding Elroy Traver into the search."

"Shit, man. Not cool." He heard Dec repeat his words to someone in the background. Probably Simon, if he was a betting man.

"Yeah. He suspects me now too."

A low whistle crept over the line. "What'cha gonna do about that?"

Charlie let out a long breath, the first since leaving his house. "Well, I left Colin to watch over him and told him to have fun."

"You do realize Colin's not always the most stable guy in his shifted forms?"

The concern in Dec's voice did little to change Charlie's mind about sicing their friend on Roy. "He'll be fine. I'm not concerned."

"Hang on, let me put you on speaker. Simon has something."

Charlie listened to the rustle of Dec moving the phone closer to wherever Simon was.

"Hey, Charlie. I think I've got something for you. Looks like there's a private firm backing this so-called task force. Doesn't look like it's officially on the books."

"What firm?"

"The Nightingale Group. I've never heard of them before, though. Hold on."

The subtle clicks of Simon's fingers on the keyboard echoed over the phone line.

"Hold on." Dec's command halted the typing sound. "Go back."

The silence hung thick.

"Charlie, how far away are you? I think you might need to come see this."

He pulled a u-turn in the middle of 519 after briefly checking his mirrors, and sped towards Belvidere. "What is it?"

"You are going to need to see this for yourself," Dec answered and followed it with another low whistle.

"I'll be there in fifteen." Pedal to the floor, he disconnected the call as the truck lurched forward. Charlie turned on the lightbar. Barns and fields flew by in his peripheral vision as he neared the fork that led downtown.

Less than five minutes later, he stomped up the steps to Dec's apartment. The door opened before he even had the chance to raise his hand to knock.

"This might be a bigger thing than you thought. The Nightingale group has their hands in a lot of pies, man. One of which was financially backing Sophia George's healing arts studio over twenty-five years ago."

"What?" Charlie stopped dead in his tracks. No. That couldn't be right.

"See for yourself," Simon offered and moved from the chair in front of the computer so Charlie could sit. "From the looks of it, she took an initial investment from them to the tune of fifty grand. And when I started digging around to see what the collateral was, I couldn't find anything other than this..." Simon reached in front of him and clicked the touchpad to reveal a picture of Sophia George and Grae, as a baby, with a man he'd never seen before.

"Who's that?" He pointed at the man in the image.

"Joseph George. Gracelynn's dad," Simon supplied. "Looks like he's somehow intertwined with Nightingale. After a little more searching, his name turned up on some recent paperwork. Looks like he's not only on the board of the organization, but part of the founding family. This can't be good..."

"What?" Charlie scanned the text on the screen and found what Simon must've been talking about. "Shit. He has a reward for his missing wife and daughter? How can he say they're missing? They've been here forever. Grae was born here," he added.

"Well, based on what this says, Nightingale was created to help find the missing and exploited women and children of the world. But if you read between the lines, it sounds more like they look for pockets of unexplainable phenomena and use those reports to track paranormal creatures," Simon explained as he dropped into a squat to be on level with the screen.

"Let me look." Dec pushed his shoulders between them, nearly knocking Simon to the ground, and scrolled the screen back to the top. A few keystrokes later, and they were looking at a screen full of email communications.

"What'd you do?" Charlie asked, afraid to hear the answer. "Wait. Don't tell me if it's not legal. I'm still a cop."

"Okay, so let's just pretend we stumbled into the email account," Dec suggested. "There are emails dating back as far as... The start of email existence," he finished.

"Wait, go back." Simon pointed at a series of email threads. "There's a whole thread of messages dating back to the beginning of the month. Look." His index finger tapped the screen. "Something happened around the end of October. Something major by the looks of it."

Charlie slumped in the chair. "Yeah. Grae turned twenty-five and came into her powers." The room got quiet.

"You sure?"

"Yeah. She's a Halloween baby. Used to have costume parties all the time as a kid."

"But how does that relate to the murders?" Simon sat back on his heels.

"Apparently, Sophie was concerned that Grae's dad would come looking for her. I'm not exactly sure why, but she was pretty insistent he was involved somehow." Charlie rolled the seat away from the computer and rose to his feet. "Can we tell where the photo was taken?"

"We can run it through some searches and see if anything turns up," Dec offered. "But it looks pretty generic. Trees. Lots of them. And the rock formation looks like maybe they're up on a mountain or something. But around here, those kinds of things are pretty common."

"Shit. I know where this was taken. Jenny Jump."

19

Random Thought # 58 - The possibility of feeling your heart in your throat only occurs when your heart has been ripped from your body and stuffed back in.

❧

If there was ever a time when Charlie wished he could do more than hear people's thoughts, it was now. Distance always played a limiting role in his gift—one he'd agonized over for years when cases called for finding missing persons.

The roads leading to the state park lands were as curvy as the rest in town, but somehow felt more dangerous when he pictured Grae somewhere along their path. He slowed into a wide turn, only to press the accelerator back to the floor coming out of it. The ache in his chest returned with a vengeance. Whatever Grae had done earlier seemed to pass without a permanent impact.

Knowing she needed him, he pushed the truck harder down the roads. His mate needed him. Hell, he needed *her*. And if something happened to her on his watch, he wouldn't be able to live with himself. Possibly in the literal sense of the words.

His phone rang and he slowed the truck to pull it from his pocket. "Latham."

"Hey, I might have something for you." Colin's deep voice rose with excitement. "I might've had a little talk with our friend here."

"And?" Impatience leaked into Charlie's tone without his consent.

"Well, looks like the dump sites at Jenny Jump coincide with a brief the task force was given. Sounds like the group funding it has been scouring the area on the belief that old Ghost Lake is at the epicenter of some paranormal activity. Apparently, the legend they were told includes a husband drowning his wife in the lake for being a witch. But since then, the family has been haunted by her spirit. She's been said to take over the bodies of female descendants and use her powers to hurt the men in their life. Supposedly, the only way to remove her spirit from a body is to drown the woman in the same place her soul was cursed."

"Shit."

"I know. Creepy, right?"

"No. I know why they're taking the women there. They're trying to find who's a witch and submerge her. The other women just drown and die."

"What can I do? Want me to meet you out there?"

"Nah. Keep an eye on Roy. But can you call Isaac and let him know where I'm headed? Maybe he knows something we don't about Grae's father."

"Can do. What about Simon? He could bring Elms out in case Grae needs medical—"

"Don't say it. She's going to be okay," Charlie interrupted. "But maybe it's not a bad idea."

"Maybe I should come and give you a little muscle when it comes to going up against the crazies. I could bring Elroy, and maybe he could get through to them."

"All right. Thanks, Colin. Did Roy have anything else to offer?"

"Only that they think she's a witch. Crazy, huh? It's like a modern-day witch hunt."

"Maybe we should bring a real witch to the fight," Charlie mused aloud.

"What?"

He heard the confusion in Colin's tone. "Nothing. Thanks for the update, man." Charlie added, before disconnecting. He had to reach out to the witch who owed him a favor. He slowed the truck and pulled over to the side of the road to search through his phone.

"Hello?"

He'd almost forgotten how downright enchanting Calliope Dewsberry's musical voice was. "Callie? It's Charlie Latham."

"Oh." Her breath caught on the other end of the line. "Does he know?"

"No. I'm calling about something else."

"Oh, good. In the back of my mind, I always thought the next time I heard from you, it'd would be to tell me Colin regained his memories."

"Not this time. But speaking of those things," he hesitated, uncertain how to proceed.

"She's doing well. Someday though, she'll have some explaining to do," Callie supplied, saving him the uncomfortable questions

"Should I ask?" He checked over his shoulder and pulled back onto the road.

"I'd prefer if you didn't." Her genuineness rang through and silenced him.

"Then I won't. But I might need a favor." He eased the accelerator this time, careful to pay attention to both the call and the road.

"I'm sure I owe you at least three or four, so let's cross one off." She chuckled before falling back into her serious tone. "What's going on?"

"A friend has been kidnapped. I think the people who took her believe she's a witch," he explained.

"Am I correct in assuming she's not?"

"You are. She's an Elemental," he confided.

"Like you?" A pregnant pause followed her question.

He waited another beat to think through the ramifications of what he was about to confess. "Yes."

"Colin too, huh?"

"That's for him to answer."

"Understood." The line hung silent between them for a long minute. "So this supposed witch...what can I do to help her?"

"I'm not sure. It's for a case, but the people behind her kidnapping have been killing women that evidence points to as being potential witches, and I think they intend to drown the woman they currently have."

"Ah, they're going old school."

The pain in her voice worsened the ache in his chest. "Yeah, at least, that's my best guess based on what we've uncovered. And I can't take this to the rest of the force. Who'd believe me?"

"Okay. Where do you need me?"

"Ghost Lake." He turned the truck onto Shades of Death Road as the sun sank low behind a cloud and cast an eerie darkness on the road before him.

"You know that place is haunted, right?"

"It's all local lore. You can't be scared of a few stories people tell in the dark." A witch of her caliber could go up against devils, but worried about some fabled ghosts? He shook his head and tried another attempt. "Callie, I've been all up and down this part of Jenny Jump and never had an issue."

"Look. I owe you, so I'll pay up, but I'm bringing back-up. Last time I was around powerful spirits, I had my body taken over. It's not as fun as it sounds." She spoke in a deadpan tone which was unusual for the spirited witch.

"Deal. I'll take all the magical help I can get," he agreed. "When can you meet me there?"

"I'm at The Dews with Jason. Let me close up, get Daphne on board, then we'll be there."

"Colin's Daphne?" His stomach somersaulted. His friend chose not to remember the half-devil, half-witch he'd fallen for while saving her from the Jersey Devil not long ago, but Charlie couldn't bring himself to force the two into a reunion right now.

"She's the only Daphne I know," Callie retorted. "Besides, if the people looking for witches get a load of her in her devilish form, there's a good chance they won't be a problem for much longer."

She was right. If they all worked together and combined their gifts, they stood a chance of getting Grae back in one piece.

"Okay. Just be aware, Colin is also coming. Will that cause a problem?"

"I don't think so," she answered, but Charlie heard the doubt at the edge of her words.

They disconnected as he neared the lake and he steered the truck to the narrow shoulder of the road. The lake caused a unique fog formation in this part of the road due to the lower altitude of the surrounding mountains. People reported seeing figures, ghostly presences, that materialized out of the fog and disappeared almost as seamlessly. He'd never put much stock in those accounts over the years, but sitting there in the silence, he could almost sense the spirits people claimed haunted this stretch of road.

Using his gift, he sought any living brain patterns to calm his rising anxiety. Relief flooded his system when one particular brain patter bounced back at him.

Grae.

Alive. Not well, but alive. Adrenaline rushed through his veins as his body lurched toward the door.

Charlie? Her voice sounded like an angel's sent straight from heaven.

Grae. I'm here. I'm going to save you. Don't worry. He pushed the messages back along their mental connection.

No. Don't come out here.

You were drugged or something. I lost you. And I'm not about to lose you again.

Listen to me, Charlie. I wasn't drugged. I'm fine. Trust me. Stay wherever you are, and keep hidden. I don't want to anger him.

Him, who? Your father? His ire rose. What woman didn't want a man to come rushing in to save her? Of course, it would be his woman. He suppressed the eye roll that threatened and concentrated on the relief of knowing his headstrong mate was still alive.

20

Random Thought # 389 - If a bear poops in the woods, you should watch where you step so you don't end up in deep shit.

Gracelynn cut off her telepathic communication with Charlie and focused on the man before her. The familiarity she expected at meeting her father never hit. She supposed being strangers created distance, even among family. The ride to this place hadn't revealed much about the man who'd helped give her life, but she didn't get the feeling he was going to hurt her. At least, not yet.

JENI BURNS

"What are we doing here?" She moved slowly
through the fog that settled in the valley. This place
brimmed with life; it vibrated in the air around her,
powerful and full of excitement. She reached with her
gift to ascertain how many people waited in the mist,
but the only brain patterns she found were Charlie's
and her father's.

Odd. She swore there were more people under the
blanket fog cover.

"This place is sacred to our family." Opening his
arms wide, he stopped before a lake she hadn't noticed. "The women in our family are cursed," he explained. "And it's here they can rid themselves of their
demons."

"Demons?" Her pulse jumped, and her stomach
bottomed out. "I have no idea what you're talking
about," she hedged and mentally reached for Charlie's
steadfast support.

"Your mother knew. I'm pretty sure she had them
too. Only I never realized until after you were born.
She spent your first few nights hovering over your crib
waiting for you to perform."

"Perform?" Perplexed, she cocked her head to the
side and studied the man. He didn't look delusional,
but he surely sounded batshit crazy. No Elemental
child performed as a baby. There was no reason for her
mom to sit by her cribside as he described.

"Magic. Don't think I don't know what you are. I
knew the moment the doctor placed you in my arms.
Your eyes glowed gold, and your smile charmed even
me into believing you might be an exception." He
slowly stepped closer as if inspecting her. "When I
brought you here and asked your mother to allow me
to complete the ritual, she showed her true nature.
Within minutes, I could barely hold on to my memory

of you. I had only a single picture of you both. She must've overlooked it when she erased my memory." He got quiet. "Either that, or your mother wanted me to know what I'd lost," he whispered. "Witches are known to be vindictive, and I'd been so bold as to demand your safety from their kind."

"I'm not a witch," she objected, the word 'witch' dry on her tongue. "Neither was my mom."

"Oh, yes,she was," he insisted, putting his hands on her shoulders.

His breath smelled of tobacco and distrust as she shrank from his touch. "Really. I can't do anything special," she insisted as her brain raced for a more convincing argument. Despite being a half-breed, keeping the community's sworn secret took over. Self-preservation took a backseat to protecting the hundreds of people who hid in plain sight. She might've never been a welcome addition to the people of Harmony, but she refused to betray them even if it saved her life.

"Prove it." A dare wrapped in demand.

Narrow eyes stared her down as she threatened to falter under his scrutiny. "How?" Her brain came up empty. Nothing she could say would convince him of her humanness. She'd lie and die to protect people who'd abandoned her. But her mother would finally be proud.

"Step into the water. The essences of the witches before you will reveal the truth."

She winced as he grabbed her arm and dragged her toward the water's edge. "No. Stop." She hated the bite of panic in her words.

Grae? I'm coming. Help is here.

"No!" The cry was meant for both Charlie and her father. Whatever her father had planned, if he found out there were more people like her, he'd never stop his search—especially if he was the monster behind the deaths.

She dragged her feet but moved toward the water. Worst case? Maybe her water nature would kick in and give her a fighting chance.

"You're my flesh and blood. I wouldn't hurt you."

The fingernails digging into her flesh disagreed. "Okay, I'll do it. Whatever you want. Please, let go. You're hurting me." She winced.

He released her arm and pushed her into the shallow water. Cold water rushed into Isaac's too large boots, soaking the bottoms of the borrowed pants, and chilling her on initial contact. She shivered.

The brush of Charlie's brain met hers. She searched the surrounding area again. Two unknown female brain patterns and one unknown male. Oh, and an animal that was seemingly focused on her. Colin? What was he doing here, and what form was he in? She recognized the underlying pieces of his brain, but this time she didn't get the loyal and friendly edge his chocolate lab form had given off. No. Now, brute strength accompanied his humanity. Angry ferocity.

A lumbering shape emerged from the shadows as Charlie and his posse stayed hidden. The breath froze in her lungs. A big black bear ambled toward them. Growing up in this area, she wasn't a stranger to the beasts, but reading all those warning signs did little to prepare her for this moment. She wracked her brain. Step one… *What the hell was step one when you encounter a bear? Shit.* Panic bubbled in her gut. She grabbed the thread and remembered. Step one, don't panic. *Well, shit.* She was screwed. The bear ambled closer, inspecting the people in his path.

Stop freaking out. Colin's there to distract your dad. Give you a chance to get away. Charlie's voice sounded in her head, a welcome distraction.

The bear ambled forward. Her father moved into the water beside her. "Stay still. They aren't known for attacking people," he said, his voice low and steady.

The bear's head swung from side to side, his nose in the air. Catching their scent, his lips pulled back, teeth bared. A rumbling hiss sent her flight response into full gear. She couldn't fathom why they weren't running for their lives.

She closed her eyes as the bear neared, his breath hot on the hand at her side. The impulse to scream warred with the rationale that begged her to stay calm and composed.

"Fuck!" Charlie's curse started her.

He emerged from the trees, a small group of people at his back. The bear stopped and swung its head toward the newcomers. Gracelynn chided herself. Colin. The bear was Colin. He wouldn't hurt her. Even though he was close enough for her to stroke the soft fur on his neck or rip out her throat. A shiver shook her steadfast stance.

One of the women behind Charlie raised her hands into the air and fluttered her fingers as if weaving something in the space above her head. A low chant followed from the man at her side.

"Stop where you are," her father yelled and grabbed Gracelynn tight.

A cold chill raced up her spine at the contact. Whispers from unseen minds caressed her brain like a lover stroking her. Tender, yet urgent. A rustle behind her in the water forced her stomach into her throat and sent her pulse racing. Prickling sensations washed up her skin as if the water claimed her as its captive and dragged her into its dark depths.

Cold seeped through her clothes and unseen fingers grabbed at her—coaxing, tugging, demanding her submission. Panic crept through her body, wrapping its sharp talons into her skin as the spirits surrounded her. A wall of water rose from the lake's surface, latched onto her, and dragged her beneath.

Struggling only hastened her descent into the frigid waters. The voices in her head quieted as water rushed into her ears, blocking out the rest of the world. Eyes frozen wide, she gasped as her father's hands plunged into the water where she'd stood only moments before. His fingers wiggled before her—touching nothing, only water. Yet still touching her.

Shit.

Not again.

∿

"*She's so pretty.*"

"*But pretty isn't smart. Look, she wound up here with us.*"

"*She looks waif-ish. Doesn't she eat? Someone should get her something to eat.*"

"*Hush. You're scaring her.*"

A gentle brush of molecules stroked through Gracelynn's essence and sent a shiver though each separate droplet of her being. This whole Elemental form experience was downright confusing. Of all the things her mother had kept from her, this was the one she wished hadn't been on the list. The sensation of both existing everywhere, and simultaneously nowhere, felt as comfortable now as her favorite yoga pants.

"*What's your name, gorgeous?*"

Try as she might, Gracelynn couldn't seem to find the words to speak her name.

"Ah, Gracelynn? Such an interesting name," the voice replied to her unspoken answer. *"Don't worry. It takes some time to get your bearings,"* the voice soothed as a warmth slid through her being.

"She's one of us, is she? Then why isn't she singing?"

Singing? Gracelynn let go of herself and embraced her new form, luxuriating in the knowledge that, somehow, she belonged here.

"Yes, dear, we sing. How else do you think we get what we need?"

As if reborn, Gracelynn became aware of the beings surrounding her in the shallows. Earlier, she'd assumed they were spirits, but she was pleased to find she was wrong. Each of the voices belonged to a delicate creature with long flowing hair and wispy figures.

With every gentle movement, Gracelynn found herself more bewitched. Captivated came to mind. She imagined herself truly belonging here, with these powerful creatures. As if her thoughts were wishes, all her molecules drew together to shape her into a form similar to that of the surrounding women.

"Goodie!"

"See, I told you she was one of us," another responded.

With a cohesive shape, she felt whole again. Her life made sense, even if only for the first time. Happenings above the surface held no meaning. This moment dominated her existence, playing out like a movie. The beautiful creatures. The melodic sounds of their voices. The lack of requiring breath. The voices no longer belonged only in her head, and her ears functioned, her hearing pinpoint beneath the watery surface.

"Is this how Water Elementals shift?" She drew her hand in front of her face so she could fully examine her new body.

"Elementals? Dear, we're Sirens."

The creature before her cocked her head to the side as if waiting for her reaction.

"Sirens? Aren't they mermaids?"

"Silly human words to explain what they can't understand," scoffed one of the creatures, her bright blue eyes blazing. "We've never been as simple as those...*fish*." Distaste coated her words, and her pert little nose wrinkled. "Did you hear that? She doesn't even know what she is! Preposterous."

"Hush. She's lived longer on land than any of us have," the seeming leader argued. "Come, dear. What brought you to us?"

Gracelynn considered her words carefully. She suspected telling them she'd been brought here against her will wouldn't go over well, considering the reaction to her earlier misstep.

"It's only recently that I've been drawn to the water," she admitted.

"Only recently? That's silly."

"Beth, stop giving the poor girl a hard time," the leader reprimanded. She turned to Gracelynn, extended her arms and offered, "I'm Jenny. I'm the original Siren here. Banished long ago by my beloved. For centuries since, the men in his family have brought women here they've suspected to be witches or...for worse reasons."

"What?"

"The worst were the poor women who only had the gall to oppose one of them. All men are headstrong bastards, if you ask me," Jenny complained, shaking her head.

"Truly," agreed Beth. "All I did was sing a simple love song to engage my lover in a little post-baby enjoyment, and straight to the lake I was sent." She tsk-tsked as her fists clenched at her sides. "All under the guise of a romantic picnic *I* had to prepare."

"Unconscionable," Jenny agreed. "The men we chose were atrocious bigots. Instead of embracing the magic we offer, they turn their noses up at what they can't understand. Our magic offers the gift of everlasting love. Imagine that—love men don't have to work for. Uncomplicated, unending, unimaginably sensual love."

The twinkle in the older Siren's eyes heated Gracelynn's face. Thoughts of Charlie's attraction raced through her mind. No wonder he burned so hot and cold when it came to her. Without her knowing, she'd bewitched him into thinking whatever bond he felt was real. Dread settled deep in her soul as shame washed over her. She was a monster. Her entire life had been one giant wish to be special, and now, she was. Too bad being special meant she might've tricked the object of her affection into loving her.

"Why love?" she asked as bile threatened to rise in her throat.

"Why not, dear? At the core of our being, we want to perpetuate our species. To do so, we need viable men. The unfortunate reality however, is that male heirs are far more common than females, and once a female has given birth, she can no longer hide her nature. The cry of her newborn brings out everything she's kept under control," Jenny explained before taking Gracelynn's hand and pulling her farther into the lake's depths. "Have you found love yet, dear?"

The affirmative almost spilled from her lips before reality exploded in her mind. She thought loving Charlie would be simple and easy. They shared history. They knew each other's weaknesses. And now that she was a bona fide member of the community, nothing stood in the way.

Except, while her feelings may be real, Charlie's couldn't be. Not with her newfound gifts of persuasion.

"I don't think so," she replied when Jenny stopped pulling her through the water.

"Well, we're sunk then," Beth grumbled from behind her.

"What?" Confusion lanced through her.

"It's nothing, dear. We've been stuck here for a long time."

"How so? Last time I shifted, all I had to do was think about being human again and it happened."

"It's not so simple." Jenny released her hand.

"Those bastards claim to love us but force us here, leaving us to fend for ourselves. Abandoning us after we've given them such gifts." Beth's scowl appeared permanently etched on her face. "And they said they loved us, but the only way a Siren can regain her legs is if the man she's given her heart to wishes for her return in the place he stashed her."

A chill raced up Gracelynn's spine. *Shit.* She was as trapped as they were. Never would her father will her return, not after this blatant confirmation of her inhumanity.

Beth was right. They were sunk.

21

Random Thought # 958 - An army of one with love as their strength can overpower even the mightiest of foes.

Everything went to shit.

Grae disappeared into the water without a trace; her father let out a rebel yell; and Colin shifted back into his human form and set eyes on the witches and Daphne Barren, before stomping off into the darkness. Anger radiated from Charlie's friend, but this wasn't the moment for a heart-to-heart conversation.

"Those eyes. I know those eyes," Daphne cried out.

Charlie's heart sank as his back-up dwindled by losing one more person.

Jason and Callie stopped their spell-casting. Their brain patterns turned from attack to retreat as the half-devil, Daphne, tore through the trees after Colin. A mouthed *sorry* from Jason before they left was all he had.

Charlie knew they'd never find Colin, though. He'd shifted into his Wind nature and taken off toward home, leaving Charlie the only person standing between rescuing Grae and losing her.

Gathering his courage, a plan morphed into place in his mind. If he could convince her father she wasn't a witch, he stacked the odds in favor of saving her.

His pulse thundered in his ears. Grae's dad stood knee-deep in the water, but she wasn't anywhere in sight. Words clogged Charlie's throat, her name a dead prayer on his lips. He reached with his mind for the familiar warm touch of hers. Nothing. No response. His heart ached while his brain attempted to rationalize the situation.

As her father moved toward the shore, they locked eyes.

"What have you done?" Charlie's hand brushed the cool metal handle of his firearm at the waistband of his jeans.

"I've done what was necessary. You should thank me." The older man shook his head and continued his forward momentum until he was almost within striking distance. "You were bewitched, boy. It's happened to the best of us." Raising his hands, he paused his movement. "Did you know what she was?" The lines around his eyes deepened while he spoke. "My family has hunted these witches for years. They pretend to be human, but they aren't. Sophie kept my daughter from me. She plucked her out of my life and my memories. All because she knew we'd created a monster. But I can't let them live. It's my duty to carry on the family legacy now. And I do it willingly."

Dipping inside the man's thoughts reminded Charlie of his mother's Jell-o molds—soupy, hard to digest, and full of weird obstacles he needed to navigate around. Deep in Joseph's mind, Charlie discovered the life raft of his hatred. The thing the man clung to so tightly that his entire world had been tethered to it.

Any traces of love for Sophie or Grae were eerily absent, but what Charlie did find, stopped his world from turning.

Mermaids who lured men to their bed with the promise of true love, only to use them for the sole purpose of creating more of their kind. Women who, when confined to a body of water, couldn't leave without the blessing of their supposed love. Images of old texts— transcribed legends—blurred before his mind's eye.

One picture stood brighter against the rest. Sophie in her kitchen, making tea, fear etched on her face. Charlie watched the memory as if it were a silent film. A man's hands grabbed the community's healer, dragged her to the ground, and beat her senseless. No water nearby, there was no reason for her death other than revenge. He experienced the man's rage, heated and sharp, an instrument of pure destruction. Then a wash of guilt flowed over him.

Guilt he could work with.

"Sir, I need you to put your hands in the air and walk towards me," Charlie demanded, his voice thick with the bravado fitting of his position.

"No. I need to see for myself." Joseph turned back to the water, as if expecting to see his daughter's body break through the surface.

"You realize your wife wasn't a witch? She also wasn't a mermaid, or whatever you think your daughter is."

"She was something terrible. An abomination. She erased so much of my life." The man's voice quivered.

"She was something, but it wasn't terrible. She spent her life raising that woman into a fine human being. She lost sleep caring for people who had nowhere else to turn. She gave every bit of herself so others could find peace. If she turned on you, I'm one to think it had more to do with you." Charlie raised his gun in the man's direction before repeating his orders. "Hands in the air and walk toward me."

"You might not want to believe this, but I did the right thing. My daughter had to die. She would've been like all the others."

"What others? Those trapped here over the years?" He knew he'd struck a nerve when the man swung to face him. "Your daughter isn't a mermaid. She's something very special—powerful, even. She's one of a kind, and you won't hurt her anymore." His finger slid inside the trigger guard, ready to kill this man where he stood.

"Killing me won't bring her back." The man stepped toward the water's edge. The silence in the low valley grated on Charlie's senses. "Only he who loved her enough to bring her here can welcome her back, and I'll go to my grave without letting her free." The man took another step, landing him in the water.

Charlie wavered. If the man spoke the truth, killing him wouldn't help Grae, but he also couldn't let him get away. Before he could pull the trigger, the man disappeared.

At a full sprint, Charlie splashed into the cold water, reaching with his mind for a trace of either Grae or her father. Emptiness answered. Once he reached knee-depth, something pulled him down, and the bottom of the lake appeared to wash out beneath him. Before comprehension kicked in, his gun was wrestled from his grasp and his head submerged without a last breath.

Fear claimed control of his thoughts. He fought the hold keeping him down to no avail, and kept his eyes peeled for the perpetrator, but only found Grae's father, a mirrored panic on his weathered face.

This was it. Trying to protect the woman he was meant to love showed him nothing but the broken reality of his utter failure. She needed more than him. She needed someone stronger. She deserved to live. He deserved this death.

Charlie closed his eyes against the events playing out before him in this watery grave. Her father had doomed her. And now, Charlie would disappear with her.

The pounding in his chest subsided and his lungs tired of struggling to contain the small bit of air trapped inside. With his last conscious thought, Charlie reached for Grae one last time.

"I love you, Grae. You've always been mine. Sorry I couldn't say it earlier. I didn't know how."

22

Random Thought # 11 - Overthinking and over-loving walk hand-in-hand.

Splashing brought Gracelynn back to the present. Someone had entered the water, and she hoped against all hope it was Charlie. Even at her worst moments, he came to mind. Despite all her reservations, her love for the man ran deep.

In the instant it took to search out the source of the splashing, Beth, Jenny, and the other unnamed Sirens flowed toward the man...no...men who fought against the water's pull. Charlie and...her father. *Shit.*

"Wait," she called as the Sirens surrounded the men, stealing their breath, toying with them. "No!" She yelled against the ripples in the water. "Not him."

Her legs seemed frozen in place, unable or unwilling to propel her toward the man she'd never known, and the man she'd always loved.

Her brain raged against indecision.

The father she wanted to understand, or the man she loved enough to let go.

Shit.

She was weak—destined to desperately want what she could never have. She wasn't an Elemental. She wasn't Charlie's mate. She wasn't anything anymore.

Her shoulders slumped against the weight of her thoughts, until an errant whisper slid through her mind and hit home.

"I love you, Grae. You've always been mine. Sorry I couldn't say it earlier. I didn't know how."

His words in her head and heart acted as the accelerant she needed. He loved her. Before this moment. Before the bar. Before sleeping together. Always. He said *always.*

Her feet kicked against the water until she shook the others away from her mate. Glancing at his closed eyes, she touched the face she'd look at for the rest of her life.

Once, a long, long time ago, he'd told her she belonged to the community as much as any other member did. Then he'd kissed her until she was dizzy and ready to believe every word he promised. Now it was her turn to return the favor. She put her mouth on his and replaced the emptiness in his lungs with her breath. She gave him everything she had to offer before swimming behind him and wrapping her arms around his chest to drag him to the surface. She managed to get him safely on land before her own breath dried in her chest.

Something about the water called her back. A promise of life.

She resisted even as her chest ached. Charlie's life was in her hands. He'd been so many things to her over the years. He couldn't die because of her. Her cupped hands compressed his chest as she'd learned in a CPR course. Water gurgled from his mouth on the last compression and she dropped her head to his chest. His heart beat, but she couldn't feel the familiar puff of breath against her face when she leaned over him. Two puffs of air were all she had left inside.

Falling to the ground beside Charlie, she yearned to have the words to tell him she'd tried. She'd given her all and repaid his lifetime of favors, but darkness clawed at her insides as sweet oblivion took hold and dragged her into the unknown.

Random Thought # 92 - A simple kiss can start a fire burning so bright that anything seems possible.

Charlie woke to find himself lying on the cold ground, wrapped in the sweetest warmth he could imagine. He inhaled the fresh night air and placed a tender hand on Grae's head. But something wasn't right. She was still. Too still.

He rolled to his knees and lowered his head over her breast, listening for sounds of life. But he couldn't hear her heartbeat or the whoosh of air in her lungs.

"Grae?" He shook her shoulder as silent prayers tickled his brain.

"She needs to return. Please, sir, return her to us," a voice begged. "She belongs to us now."

Charlie looked up and locked eyes with a woman. She appeared to be young, possibly in her thirties, with long flowing locks and aquamarine eyes. His heart somersaulted. Grae couldn't belong to them, she was his. "No."

"Sir, I implore you. Return her to the waters so she may live." She swam closer to the water's edge, but kept most of her body submerged.

Protective, he gathered Grae in his arms and hugged her tight to his chest. "She doesn't belong to you. She belongs with me."

"Sir, I beg to disagree. She's Siren. She needs the waters to live, and the only way to regain her human form comes as a result of forgiveness from the man who cursed her here." The woman raised her hand from the water and up popped other feminine faces.

"That man is dead. He can't break the curse, but I'm her destined mate. Tell me how to break the curse." The thought of losing her before they truly began added to the ache growing in his chest.

"The curse of a Siren can only be cured with the breath of air from their beloved," the woman in the water sniped. "Return her to us now of your own free will, or we will make it so."

The threat landed hard against his ears. Surely a bunch of creatures confined to the waters of this lake couldn't compel him to hand over the only person he'd ever loved. Charlie shook his head and stood to his full height. If Grae needed breath, he'd give her his. Instead of dipping his face to hers, he shed his clothes and adopted his Wind nature. As the transformation overtook him, a chorus of voices rose from the surface of the water.

Their words held no meaning to him as he aimed to surround Grae with his essence. But the rising voices combined in a seductive melody, tugging at every emotional impulse in his transformed being. The draw to their song pulled him away from his purpose.

Unable to resist them in his Elemental form, he regrouped back to his body and settled by Grae once more. "Forgive me, love. I don't want to return you to them, but I need you too much to let you die." He pressed a kiss to her cold lips and brushed long, dark strands away from her face. "I'd give you my last breath, Gracelynn George, if I thought it would save you. I'd give you anything." He lifted her into his arms and carried her into the shallows. In the light of the moon, she appeared as peaceful as a sleeping child. But as he lowered her to the surface, his heart began to tear into a thousand pieces.

The leader of the Sirens swam to where he stood and gripped Grae's arm.

"Let her go. We'll care for her."

His fingers refused to relax their grip as the water soaked them again. Grae's eyes opened and breath escaped her lips.

"Charlie? You're okay?"

Joy exploded in his chest as her hazel gaze burrowed into him. "Yes. I'm fine. Just having a hard time letting you go, even though I know I need to." He lowered his head and grazed her lips with his.

"Come now, it's time for her to fully return to the water," the Siren at her side demanded.

"No. She's fine. See?" He barely glanced at the creature vying for his woman. His eyes remained locked on the lips he wanted to kiss for the rest of eternity.

"It's the water. She needs it to live now." The woman tugged, and Grae began to slip from his grasp.

"Charlie?"

"Shh, love. This crazy woman believes you're a Siren and need to stay in the lake. Something about your father being the only one who can break the curse keeping you here." The words died on his lips when she broke eye contact and lowered her lashes. "It can't be true. You're a Water Elemental. We've seen the proof already. Don't let her convince you different."

"I'm sorry, Charlie. My father's family wasn't full of half-breed Waters. It was full of Sirens. The bond you think we have might not even be real. I might've inadvertently spelled you into believing you're in love with me. Apparently, it's something Sirens do." She touched his face. "I've loved you for so long, Charlie. It only makes sense I'd want you to be mine."

The feel of her fingertips on his cheek started a heat boiling deep in his gut. She was wrong, and he'd prove it even if it killed him. Wrenching her from the Siren's hold, he tossed her over his shoulder so that only her toes and hair grazed the water as he waded back to the shore. Grae struggled in his arms, but a quick pat on her butt quieted her. "I need you to trust me, Grae. For years I've taken a tonic to help offset the bonding process because, that night around the campfire, I knew you were the only woman for me. I've loved you from afar for most of my life and I'm not about to believe it was all for nothing. I'm sure there's something at your mom's studio that can help you too. I'll call Elms and have her meet us there. We'll fix you."

No sooner had they left the water, when Grae began struggling for breath again.

"You'll only hurt her if you take her away," the Siren called. "If you love her, you'll leave her here where she belongs."

He stopped short. If the Siren was right, he wouldn't make it to the clinic before Grae died. He knelt to the ground and sat her beside him. He cupped her chin in his hand and tipped it back. "I'm going to go look for a fix. I need you to stay close enough to the water to breathe, but don't go in. Please. I can't lose you again." Desperate, he ran through the Siren's declarations. His breath. Without a moment to lose, he dipped his head toward her and began the mouth-to-mouth part of his emergency responder training. Her lips were cold under his. His efforts changed nothing. Drawing away, he brushed the back of his hand across her cheek. His resolve crumbled. "I won't lose you. I'll figure some way to fix this," he promised.

Her response was nothing more than a nod, but he had to believe she meant it. Despite knowing he had to get her back into the water, he needed her to feel his love. He bent and placed his lips on hers, stealing away any last breath she might've had as he kissed her deeply and lifted her into his arms once more. Every promise he ever wanted to make to her lingered in that embrace until he gently set her in the shallows.

"Promise me you'll be here when I return." Desperation clung to his words, and he hated how vulnerable he felt. Until she met his eyes and smiled.

"I'll do everything in my power to come back to you, Charlie Latham."

Her breathy words stirred a hope deep inside he'd been hesitant to believe. "You will?" His question sounded more like an affirmation.

"I've been in love with you ever since my prom," she admitted, her lashes falling to cover her eyes. "Maybe even before, if I'm being completely honest."

He grabbed her hands in his and kissed her mouth again with everything he was worth. She pulled from his kiss and smiled.

"I'll come for you, Grae. Always." He kissed her forehead and rose to his feet. Leaving her killed a piece of him. Every footstep created an invisible chasm between them. He shook the mental image from his head. Once in his truck, he shucked his soaked boots and coat. The rest would have to wait. He pointed the vehicle toward Sophie's.

A few minutes into the drive, his ringtone sounded. The button on his steering wheel connected the call. "Latham."

"Charlie? What happened to Colin? He's freaking out."

"Shit. Sorry, Elms. Was a little distracted by almost dying." He heard a little yelp over the line as his words were delivered.

"What? Are you okay?"

"Yeah. Still kicking. How's Colin?"

"Spouting off nonsense about seeing the devil, and something about knowing she's carrying his baby." A pregnant pause lingered. "Is it true?"

"It's true he met someone a little while back, but he wasn't ready to deal with what she meant to him. I'm not sure about the rest," he hedged. Knowing how close Elms and Colin were, he didn't want her to have to lie about anything. Well, that and Elms was a horrible liar. "Hey, any chance you can meet me over at Sophie's in, like, thirty minutes?"

"Sure, but will they let me in?"

"Wait until I get there, and I'll make sure they let you in." He flicked the blinker and waited for an oncoming car to make the turn, before pulling out onto the main road. Something about the car looked familiar, but he couldn't put his finger on it.

"What are we looking for at Sophie's?"

Elms' words from the phone pulled him back to reality. "I need something to help Grae. She thinks she's a cursed Siren. Anytime she sets foot outside of the water, she can't seem to breathe. There's got to be something I can do to help her."

"Wait. She thinks she's a Siren? I thought she's a half-breed Wind?"

"Until a few hours ago, it was looking more like she was a Water. There was an incident where she took on the Water form, and Isaac assumed her dad was at least a half-breed himself." The road stretched free and clear before him.

"Wow, that's strange. I know Sophie has all sorts of resources, but I'm not sure I've ever seen anything about Sirens in them. I thought they were only a legend sailors made up."

"I don't know. There's a whole damn lake of them out on Shades of Death," he argued as he turned onto River Road and headed toward his house.

"I'll see if Simon and Declan can find out anything before I head over. But Charlie, I know Gracie will be okay. I have to believe, after all your suffering, you two will have your time together. Your patience will pay off. Look at me and Simon. Fate will see you through."

Charlie disconnected the phone without a word. Fate was his people's version of a deity, and so many of them took issue with her recent rash of erratic behavior. But this would take the damn cake. If he couldn't figure out how to help Grae, there was a chance he'd never get to experience all the good parts of bonding. He pulled into his driveway and slammed on the breaks. Splayed across the doorjamb to his home lay a blood-soaked Elroy.

"Shit." Charlie shoved his feet into his wet boots, grabbed his cell, and raced to the porch. On closer inspection under the porch light, it was evident his old friend had been dead for a while. He dialed 911 and gave them the required information, then followed that call with one to his boss.

"Captain? It's Latham. Roy's dead. The George woman has been kidnapped. I called the locals for Roy, but thought you might want to meet them here at my place. I'm heading to the George place to see if I can find what the kidnappers want," he added.

"Fuck, Latham. What the hell happened?"

"I'm not sure, Captain, but I refuse to find another dead body on my watch today. I'll call in for back up if I need it."

Without waiting for confirmation, he disconnected the call and stepped around the body to get inside. His house looked intact despite the body on the front porch. Whoever killed Elroy must've only wanted *him* dead, or he feared Colin's body would've made a matched set. Charlie slipped into a change of clothes and quickly packed a duffelbag with two more—one for himself, and one for Grae. She'd need something to keep her warm once he figured out how to get her out of the lake permanently.

24

Random Thought # 783 - Being a damsel in distress isn't all it's cracked up to be.

Gracelynn hated feeling stuck. Stuck in the shallows waiting for Charlie's return. Stuck in the lake her own father cursed her to. Stuck somewhere in-between being human, Siren, and Elemental.

It didn't help that she could hear the other Sirens' thoughts. Jenny seemed aggravated by her refusal to fully enter the waters, and Beth's high horse stood taller than most skyscrapers. The word outcast kept being thrown around like confetti. Hurtful confetti.

Squaring her shoulders, she bit back a stream of angry words. It wasn't like this was her first trip to outcast island. Not only had she lived there most of her life, she even had a pretty nice cabin and knew the locals. Laughter bubbled up inside her chest as the mental image came into view. Living her life meant a careful balance between existing, and pretending the biddies of the world didn't get to her.

Tires crunching on the road beyond the trees caught her attention. Charlie hadn't been gone long enough to already be returning. She cocked her head to the side and reached with her gift.

Oh, shit.

The man from the bar. The killer looking for her. He'd found her. How?

Shit. Shit. Shit.

Her limbs shook and her chest tightened. Breath struggled to move through her body. Her father hadn't been behind her mom's death? But the glimpses she'd seen in his head featured her dead body at the crime scene. What the hell? She looked toward the middle of the lake for help, but the Sirens tossed her a good-luck-sucker look and disappeared beneath the surface without a word. It was either join them, or stay here in this vulnerable state.

Footsteps drew closer through the underbrush, sending her stomach into her throat, as tears welled behind her eyes.

"Well, well. What do we have here?"

His voice wasn't deep, but the menacing tone shook her to the core nonetheless.

"Stop there. I'll scream," she called as she inched her way farther into the waters.

"It won't do you any good, Gracelynn."

220

The sound of her name on his lips stopped her movement. "Do I know you?" She peered into the darkness until she could distinguish the outline of the man coming toward her.

"I'm the proud new owner of a magical creature."

She imagined a sneer covering his face as he stalked closer still. A length of rope hung from his hands.

"Now, do me a favor, and come nice and willingly. I don't want to have to hurt you like the others."

"Others? You mean my mom?" She scrambled to her feet, sending water sliding off her exposed body and readied herself to run, even though she had no idea where to go.

"Your mother refused to disclose your whereabouts. She made her decision." His heavy footsteps sunk in the waterlogged ground where she'd lain only moments before.

"What do you want with me?" She slid on pebbles beneath the water and floundered, before regaining her balance.

"Your magic. Don't you know? An Elemental is a rare find. They work so hard to keep their identity a secret. But you aren't just any old Elemental, are you?" He raised a knowing eyebrow. "If you were, I bet you would've shifted by now. But something has you tethered to the water, doesn't it?"

"No," she argued, but her voice shook, betraying her.

"Let me guess," he began. "Your dear old dad magically found you. Today. After all these years of having abandoned you, and what does he do? He brings you here, right?"

A chill ran up her spine. "How?"

"Half-breeds are a special anomaly. Did you know that?" He ran the rope across one of his palms. "Ones who exhibit gifts such as yours though, they are extremely rare. And unlike their full-blooded friends, they aren't tethered to the bonding process." He waded into the water. "I've waited a very long time for this moment."

She slipped on a rock, her head submerging beneath the water as she struggled to ensure the man wouldn't be able to grab her.

Gracelynn's gift kicked into full effect as adrenaline coursed unbidden through her body. This man. He knew her father. She pulled snippets from his brain without any effort. The two men shaking hands. Her father handing over cash. Her for her mother. That had been the deal. So many years ago. Before she even was old enough to walk. This man spying on her from across the wooded tree line separating her childhood home from Isaac's. He'd been a day laborer at Isaac's farm? How had she managed to avoid him this long then?

Fingers brushed the back of her thigh, and she swallowed a mouthful of lake water. Not needing to breathe, she calmed quickly, until the eyes of her father stared back at her. He was supposed to be dead. Beside him drifted a Siren she hadn't been introduced to.

He grabbed her arm and pulled her to the water's surface. No sooner had she broken through, when the other man grabbed her around the neck. Tight. She sputtered and writhed against his hold, flailing with every ounce of energy she had.

"Stop. Now," her father ordered. "Frank, get her to the grass. We can tie her up there."

"No!" Her cry was cut short as the man named Frank tightened his grip.

"Get her out of the water," her dad demanded.

"I thought you said she'd be confined to it?"

"Only until I release her." His eyes burned as he glared at her before turning his attention to the other man. "What happened with Sophie last night?"

"She refused. We talked about this. You changed the terms long ago, friend." Frank spoke through teeth gritted with effort as he wrestled to get a hold on her legs and wrap them in the rope.

"I still wanted a few minutes with her. Let her know I'd done it and broken her spell."

Her dad pulled her shoulders so far back, she worried they would snap under the pressure. A wince twisted her lips.

"How did you break the spell, Joe? I thought that witch wasn't useful."

"Ah, she came through in the end, old friend. Turns out this old dog can still be pretty persuasive when he wants to be."

Gracelynn gagged at the innuendo flying from her father's mouth as they manhandled her bared body into submission. As the last remnants of lake water slid from her skin, her breath froze in her lungs and her thoughts slowed.

"Looks like your girl isn't feeling too well."

"Oh, yeah. She takes after her grandmother, all right."

Gracelynn tried to focus on his words, but the emptiness in her mind called to her, begging, pleading.

"I release you from the Siren curse, my love."

As if an invisible chain from her to the water had been broken, she took a gulp of air into her lungs and savored the feeling of actual breathing.

"See, I told you. Bringing her here was worthwhile. She's proven herself to be a Siren," Joseph bragged before hefting her over his shoulder. "Where are you parked?"

"On the main road, just behind you."

The men strolled through the trees as if nothing was amiss. Her stomach hurt, and her head pounded from the earlier oxygen deprivation and from the position she was being carried, which sent blood pounding at her temples. She'd black out soon. She could feel the darkness calling her again. But before she let go, she thought of Charlie. Her love. Her friend. The man who never failed to save her when she needed him most.

She needed him now more than ever.

25

Random Thought # 34 - Superheroes wear capes.
Police officers wear badges and bulletproof vests. Men
in love are only armed with the desire to hold their
mate once more.

❧

Elms had beaten Charlie to Sophie's and was waiting for him as he pulled into the spot beside her in the parking area for the clinic.

"So there's a legend about Sirens that is almost crazy enough to be true," she started as soon as he opened the truck door. "Apparently, a woman who I assume was a Water, married a witch. But he was destined for great things and was sent traveling around the country to help train other witches in his craft of dream walking. As the years went by, his love for his wife grew more and more with each passing moon cycle, until he was literally mad with desire for her. He claimed he could hear her singing in his heart when he closed his eyes at night. The song supposedly drove him to seek her out in her dreams, and he wasn't pleased to find the object of his affection tangled in the arms of another."

"Wait. Hold on a sec." Charlie raised a hand to halt her verbal vomit. "What does this have to do with Grae?" He gestured for Elms to join him as he strode toward the clinic's main entrance. She fell into step beside him, her strides needing double for one of his, but she jumped back into her tale as she kept pace.

"Well, here's where it gets interesting. The witch was so angered, he cursed the Water into a lake not too far from here. Apparently, before Jenny Jump was a protected park, it was home to early settlers. But what he didn't realize is she had given birth to his child, and in cursing her, he left the child without a mother."

"Again, how does this help Grae?" he asked as he pulled open the storm door and stepped aside so she could slide the key into the lock.

Two keys later, they stepped inside. Elms ushered him into the back part of the office where the patient rooms and Sophie's office were located.

"Here's the thing," she prattled on. "The community did what it does best. It closed ranks and took care of its own. The baby grew up and had children and so on. But the witch also had more children and passed down the story of his cheating wife so all his heirs would be on-guard for deceptive Elementals who masqueraded as witches. He gifted his heirs with the abil-

226

ity to seek out Elementals. The stuff Simon found said something about hunters with the gift of sight. It wasn't clear, though, what kind of sight."

"So wait. Grae's being hunted?"

Elms sat behind Sophie's desk and opened a drawer before gesturing for him to take a seat opposite her. "It seems that way." She paused and pulled a book out of the drawer. "Sophie's been keeping journals of her dreams for years. Apparently, she had some issues with premonitions. Not always reliable ones, mind you," she added. "But it was news to me." Elms shrugged a shoulder and slid the book across the desk to him.

"Sophie told me if anything happened to Gracie, I was to give this to you. She thought it might be helpful in getting her back. She seemed to think you'd know what to do."

"Why me?" he asked as he took possession of the thick, leather-bound journal.

"Why didn't you tell me you and Gracie mated?" Elms' accusatory tone hurt.

"Isn't it kind of personal?" He opened the book and began flipping through the pages.

"I don't mean now, Charlie. How long ago did it happen?"

"What are you talking about?" He refused to have this conversation with the red-headed healer. Not now. Maybe not ever.

"The journal Sophie left included instructions to provide you with the tea she and Isaac used. Recipe. Directions for use. Clients to prescribe it for." The look on her face said more than her words. "How long, Charlie?"

"Since before I went to college." He shook his head and looked at his lap. Admitting it aloud made him feel like a fucking coward. He'd loved his woman for the better part of his life, and here he was, still scared to admit it and to allow himself to be vulnerable. Why? What did he have to gain by not admitting his feelings? The reduced risk of pain and rejection? Hell, he would lose her if he didn't find a way to save her now. Then he'd be without her and his heart for the rest of his foreseeable future.

"Wow. I thought it must've been some time, but that's longer than I imagined." She rose to her full height, which was still way too short for a grown adult, and came around the desk. "What can I do to help you get her back?"

"I need something to help her breathe out of the water. Something to break the Siren curse."

"Hmm..." Elms rubbed her pregnant belly absent-mindedly and slid between the back of his chair and a bookcase on the wall. She fingered the spines until she found the perfect one. "Okay, that's kinda what I thought," she muttered.

"What?"

"Waters and Sirens are essentially the same thing. A cursed Water might become a Siren, but she's still a Water at her core," Elms explained and laid the open text on the desk in front of him. "Look here, though." She pointed to a passage with her index finger.

A mated Water's love knows no bounds. They cannot be contained to any one form so long as their Mate is around.

"What's that supposed to mean?" He pushed the book away, his fists balling on the desk.

"It means, as long as you're there, she should be strong enough to break the curse herself, so long as you two are feeling the bond." She stopped talking and eyed him. "You are feeling the bond, right? Please, tell me you aren't still using the tea."

228

The edge of panic in Elms' voice sent sweat to his brow. "Why?"

"Charles! You can't be on the tea after you've completed the bond. The side-effects could be irreversible. How long has it been? Never mind, if you've been on this tea for any length of time, it's possible your bond isn't complete yet."

She rushed from the room, leaving him alone with his thoughts. Before he could think through what possible consequences she might be speaking of, clinking bottles announced her return.

"Here. Take these." She thrust no fewer than five vials into his hands.

"What is all this?"

"Take them. Stop asking questions. You need to fix your bond. Now. And these are the best chances you have, Charlie."

Elms definitely lacked Sophie's gentle touch when it came to the healing arts, it was a damn fact, but she made up for it in gusto. He opened each vial and drained the contents one by one. The taste on his tongue after downing the combination was less than stellar. It was downright noxious.

"What the hell? Those were meant to be mixed?"

"Well..."

"Elma." His warning tone died on his lips as his head was inundated with thoughts. Not his. Not even Elms, but...*Grae's*.

"By the look in your eyes, I'm going to assume they fixed the problem." Smug worked on the healer, but he'd never admit it.

"I think so. I can hear her." He paused and listened to the barrage of thoughts running through his mind. Every so often, his name popped up. She was thinking about him? His heart stuttered a beat.

"Good. It's the part of the bond that helps mates be apart, but in your case, because of your gift," she clarified, "I think it'll be even stronger. Can you get a read on where she is?"

"Yeah, and it's not good news. She's not still at the lake. Seems like her father didn't drown, nor was he behind the deaths. But she's in trouble."

Charlie sprang from his seat and grabbed Elms by the arms. "Any chance you have something to rescue her?"

"Yeah." Elms poked a finger into his chest. "You. You're all she needs. Trust the bond to see you through."

～

Trust the bond.

Yeah, the bond that had a tendency to make his life a disaster. Charlie shook his head as he slid behind the wheel. He swung the truck around and headed back down the drive. He got the feeling she hadn't gone far from the lake, but without knowing exactly where Grae was being held, he worried he wouldn't be able to arrive in time.

He drove fast, only partially focused on the road before him. With every passing mile, her voice became louder in his mind.

"Grae? Can you hear me?" Talking aloud in the empty car to a woman off in the distance made him question his sanity. Until she answered him back.

Charlie? Is that you? How's this even possible?

He imagined her hazel eyes glowing golden with her confusion. "Elms," he admitted.

Elms?

"Actually, it's us. The bond. It's real, Grae. Has been for years."

Impossible.

The doubt in her voice rang loud and clear in his head. "It's true. Your mom helped me suppress it. Elms undid it." He needed her to know. Needed her to understand his reasons for not wanting to bond had nothing to do with her, and everything to do with his own insecurities and fears. But this wasn't the time. Because if he didn't find her soon, he'd never have the opportunity to say the things he needed her to hear, let alone kiss her lips again and lose himself in the little moments. "Where are you, Grae? I'm coming for you."

I don't know exactly. There's a small cabin not far from the lake. They brought me here. I think my father sold me to some guy. Frank, his name is. He wants me for my gifts. Says because I'm a half-breed I'm not tethered to the bond. I think he's planning to try to start his own half-breed race. I'm scared, Charlie.

Her panicked thoughts pushed his foot on the accelerator and the truck lurched forward. "I'm coming, Grae. Hold on, baby."

Warmth spread through his thoughts like butter on hot toast.

Charlie, promise me you'll do whatever it takes to stop them.

"Of course, baby. They won't hurt you. Not now, not ever." The promise fell from his lips as if he'd been waiting for the perfect moment to utter the sentiment. His heart ached. The men holding her didn't know the hell driving towards them, ready to destroy all their plans.

"Describe where you are, Grae. What can you see?"

I don't know. I'm in a basement.

He felt a wince of pain as she struggled to crane her neck in the dark room. His abilities had never allowed

231

him to experience someone else's physical pain before, and when he realized she was bound tight to a metal chair, it held the air in his lungs hostage. Still as bare and exposed as he'd left her at the lake.

"Oh, Grae," he groaned as he white knuckled the truck around a hair-pin curve.

I'm okay, Charlie. I know you're coming for me. Be safe.

Before he could respond, a burst of pain exploded in the back of his head and Grae disappeared. Someone had hurt her.

They would pay with their lives.

26

Random Thought # 547 - White knights can't be expected to save all the princesses of the world. Some princesses need to figure out how to save themselves.

❧

When Gracelynn awoke, the ache in her head added to the pain deep in her ribs. She opened her eyes and struggled with the restraints tethering her to the cold metal chair. Tired of being held captive, she jerked against the ropes grating on her skin.

She adjusted her blurred vision until she could see a tiny window in the corner of the room. The basement smelled of mildew and dank as if it hadn't been opened and aired out in a long time. She used her gifts and attempted to discern where her father and Frank were in the small cottage. After being caught off guard and hit on the back of the head while communicating with Charlie, she needed to be more discreet.

Her brain reached the men's and she fought harder against the bonds holding her fast. Frank did, in fact, plan to use her to start his own half-breed empire.

Digging around in his head, she learned more than she bargained for. He'd been searching for her since her thirteenth birthday. Hunting her like a rare collectible and waiting to put his own half-breed seed inside her. She swallowed back the vomit threatening to wash up her throat. Her father knew this man. Knew what he wanted her for. Knew he planned to keep her locked away, popping out half-breed babies he could sell to the highest bidder.

Her stomach's fight to void won, and she choked on bile as it made its way from the core of her and landed on the floor with a splash. Her father had no love for her. He was as evil as Frank. Brokering a deal to sell one's daughter to the highest bidder did not make one even remotely close to father of the year.

She left Frank's brain and took a chance, dipping into her father's. Darkness awaited her in his head. Evil thoughts. Her mom's death displeased him, but only because he'd missed the opportunity to do the deed himself. Gracelynn's value brought dollar signs to the forefront of his mind and made her ill all over again. The connection between the men became apparent all too quickly.

Together, they'd been outcast from a community much like the one in Harmony. Elemental half-breeds weren't as much as an anomaly as she'd been told. In fact, they were more prevalent than she gathered even people like Isaac knew. She couldn't imagine these people being scattered all over the world, not knowing where they came from and coming into their gifts without any support. A chill worked its way over her body. Her father first met Frank when they took a fishing trip as teens. Both loved the water and were drawn to it as if by compulsion. Years later, they began experiencing odd behaviors and learned about the Elemental Community. However, shunning half-breeds was the norm. When her dad met her mom, Joseph took it as a sign from the universe that his destiny was to bring all half-breeds into the inner circle. But before he could even begin to make headway, his father threatened to kill his newly-pregnant wife after discovering her Elemental secret.

One fight led to another until Grae saw her father put his hands around her mother's neck. The image haunted her to no end. Her mom appeared so calm in the memory, up until a baby crawled into the room. Her. She was the baby in the memory.

In all her years of living with Sophie, she'd never been tuned into her mom's Elemental gift. In fact, she assumed it had something to do with her healing arts practice, but seeing the image play out in the dark corner of her father's brain, she saw something she never expected. Not only could her mother whip into her Wind nature in an instant, but she also called forth every feat of nature the Earth had to offer. A tornado knocked him backward as sleet pelted his skin. In the confusion, Gracelynn witnessed the last look she'd shared with the man who gave her life. His face contorted from anger and fear to outright rage. Her mother had done all she could to protect them from this man. This evil man.

She withdrew from his mind and dared attempt contact with Charlie. Closing her eyes against the darkness, she willed her mind to find the mental pathway between them. Off in the distance, she saw a golden glow. Without hesitation, Gracelynn followed the path knowing it led to him.

Unfortunately, it dead-ended before she could connect. Almost as if it were a cut power line. A jolt of pain lanced through her chest and gripped her midsection in an iron embrace. A whimper fell from her lips, determined to boil to a full-on scream against the pain.

She opened her eyes and conjured the image of Charlie. Tall, strong, silent. The scent of sandalwood she identified as him. With the image in mind, she closed her eyes again and sought the pathway, but nothing remained.

A blast from somewhere nearby sounded and a choked sob stumbled from her chest. No. *"Charlie!"* His name was a simultaneous demand and cry on her lips.

"He can't hear you," a deep voice from the back corner of the room answered.

Frank.

"Your father saw to your little rescue party," he intoned. "He always was good at long distance shots." He paused as if waiting for her to say something more. "No one will come for you now. You're mine. Together, we'll start a whole new race of Elementals. One stronger and more powerful than those pure-bloods." Disdain dripped from his words.

Pain course through her veins. Charlie couldn't be dead. Even if her father an expert marksman, there was no way Charlie would be so stupid as to come here alone. She replayed her last telepathic touch with him and decided the man couldn't be right. Charlie was far too smart to come without back up.

"Water and what?" he asked as he approached. "A Siren can only be a Water, but I get the feeling your mother wasn't one." He tipped her chin up with his index finger and stared through her. "Those eyes," he sighed. "They look like they are trying to figure out how to rip me to shreds where I stand." A chuckle echoed in the dank space. He slid his hand along her jaw until his hand caressed her cheek. "We'll produce the strongest race of supernatural creatures around. No doubt about it."

Fury built in her veins as his touch lingered on her skin. This man was old enough to be her father, and from the thoughts running through his head, she knew he didn't intend to cherish her. Far from it. She was a bitch in heat—his words, not hers. Nothing more than a vessel to start his own race of super humans.

"Grae?"

Charlie's voice landed in her head, heavy and thick as if he was struggling to stay awake. She immediately tuned out everything dealing with Frank and focused all her energy on Charlie.

"Are you okay? I thought I heard a shot," she cried across the newly-reformed pathway in her mind.

"Someone shot me. I'll be okay. I called for back-up-."

"You're hurt. I knew it. Where?"

"Don't worry, babe. I need you to focus on getting out of there. Using your Water gift to your advantage. These men aren't fully human."

"I know. Half-breeds," she agreed. *"I'm worried they can use my Water nature against me."*

"How so?"

The mental pathway dimmed as his energy waned.

"They are Waters too."

237

"Remember Grae, you've always been more than you thought. Not only to others, but to yourself. Trust that and focus."

His voice died in her head and her heart sank as the ripping in her chest restarted. She couldn't lose Charlie. Not now. They needed to make up for so much lost time and this chance wouldn't come around again.

Footsteps on the stairs pulled her away from the fading remnants of Charlie.

"Who knows you're here?" Her father's tone carried all the warning she needed.

"You shot him," she accused. "You're in big trouble now. He's a cop. And not just any old cop. He's a detective who's investigating all the recent murders." She paused to catch her breath before adding, "You know, the ones you two have orchestrated while trying to find me."

Her unveiled accusation hung in the air between the three of them.

"I'm not sure she's going to be worth all the trouble," Frank grumbled.

"You're not killing her too," her father chided. "You wanted her because of her unique mixing. We had a deal."

"The deal didn't include her already having a mate though. You said half-breeds didn't have fated mates. Yet she behaves like a mated Elemental."

"Because I am." She spat the admission at their feet and lifted her chin high. It felt amazing to own her feelings for Charlie, even if in this awful situation. She belonged to him, and everyone needed to hear it.

"We'll take her back to the lake. Confine her there," her father suggested. "She can't be mated to a human *and* cursed to the lake. She'll have no choice but to break her mated bond."

"No." She struggled against the restraints.

"Until she breaks the bond, she's no good to us," Frank complained. "How long will it take? I'm sure there's a way to force the issue."

"If the man I shot was her mate, the bond could break any time now."

"No." The single whispered word ripped from her chest in a ball of fury. Pent-up anger seeped from her pores in a twist of rage and torment. She'd spent her entire existence fighting for something out of her grasp. Not anymore.

Her blood boiled. Desperation turned to confidence somewhere deep inside her and exploded outward.

Understanding smacked her upside the head, but not until after she no longer had a human head to speak of. Instead of the flowing stream she became in water, she felt thin, light, airy. Power vibrated through her every molecule, building into a frenzy of activity. She became aware of her form as the chair she'd been tethered to only moments ago, scraped across the basement floor before it took flight. The satisfaction of seeing the once harmless object become a projectile aimed squarely at Frank's confused face sent a wave of warm reassurance through her.

The thick sound of the metal sinking into his skull gave her a reason to celebrate. His body collapsed on the floor with a thud of finality she wished she could bathe in. One down. One to go.

"Gracelynn, I command you back to the lake," her father yelled from behind the protective shield of his arms braced in front of his face.

Something deep inside roiled at his words. Obeying wasn't an option. Instead, she gathered her anger and all the resentment hidden below the surface. Everything she'd spent her entire life repressing coursed through each bit of her being.

Existing as a Wind gave her a newfound sense of exhilaration. The kind being fluid in her Water form hadn't. She twisted and twirled on herself until she possessed tornado strength. The floor above her trembled under her power. The walls of the basement quaked. Her father dropped to his knees as if it might somehow save him from the rampage she wrought. Too little, too late.

Gracelynn whipped herself faster and faster until the building exploded outward, shattering the night sky with shrapnel. She ignored the pang of guilt when she spied her father's body skewered on a metal pole in the distance.

"What was that?"

Charlie's voice throbbed in her head. Her head? Her human form lay on the cold ground, yet her awareness seemed to hover nearby, separate. What happened? She'd never heard it was possible to separate her consciousness from her body before even with the shifting. And yet, she hovered over her body, a lost soul.

"Grae?"

This time his voice washed over her senses. Blood ran down the side of his face. She longed to touch him, reassure him, and heal him, but getting her essence back into her body... Impossible.

Charlie's face collapsed and his knees buckled beside her body. "Grae, you can't leave me. Not now." He gathered her in his arms and held her body against his chest, her head cradled against his shoulder.

The metallic chirping of his phone cut the eerie stillness left in the wake of her tantrum. He wrenched it from his pocket. "Latham."

She waited while whomever was on the other end of the line spoke.

"I need your help, Elms. She's unresponsive."

He paused and tucked a strand of hair behind Gracelynn's ear.

"Take her back there? No."

Gracelynn wished she could hear the healer's side of the conversation, but unless Charlie decided to become the most redundantly chatty person on the planet, she wouldn't have an iota about what was being said. Their mental pathway gone and her energy zapped made her limited existence frustrating.

"If you think it'll work, I'll try anything. I can't lose her." The pause this time was as pregnant as the healer on the other end of the line. "I love her. It's not the bond. I've always loved her." He tucked her body against his chest and switched the cell to his other ear with a wince. "I'll need your help later too. Might've got grazed with a bullet."

A bullet? She inspected his head and saw the gash above his right ear. Sure enough, her father's bullet had been as well-aimed as Frank alluded. Panic welled inside. She needed to touch him. Soothe him. Kiss his lips and promise him forever. He pocketed the cell and lifted her limp body in his arms.

27

Random Thought # 927 - Desperate men know no limitations when it comes to the woman they love.

After settling Grae into the truck, he pulled onto the main road and headed back to the lake. Elms' might be a little unorthodox with her healing methods, but he refused to let the love of his life go so easily.

He stopped behind Simon's Maserati and jumped from the cab. Elms scurried from the passenger side of the convertible and opened his passenger door.

"If she's part Wind and part Water, one of those elements should heal her. Obviously, it seems the tornado she caused took a lot out of her. I think the lake's waters can help restore her."

"But dunking her in there last time cursed her. I don't know," he cautioned.

"Simon, can you grab my bag? I need to check her real quick." Elms gestured to her husband, then pushed Charlie back from the truck. "Look, Charlie, I know you don't want anything bad to happen to her, but I need you to trust me. Okay?"

Simon hefted a bag onto the baseboard before giving him a quick pat on the shoulder. "She's the best around, man. She won't let anything happen to Sophie's daughter." He ducked his head and moved out of the way.

"Good news and bad news," Elms called over her shoulder. "I can hear her heart beating, but no breath sounds."

"That can't be good." He scrubbed a hand across his jaw.

"It's not. Hearts don't beat for long without oxygen in the bloodstream. If she isn't breathing, she isn't getting oxygen." Elms hopped down, her eyes narrowed at him. "I'll say it once more, take her to the lake. I have a feeling the water will set things right." She waited a beat, shook her head, and turned to Simon. "Come help me get her to the water."

"No. I'll do it." The idea of another man, even one already mated, touching his mate sent a riot of jealousy through him. He slid Grae from the seat and carried her back to where this whole nightmare began.

At the edge of the water, he noticed the heads of the other Sirens near the center of the lake. "She's not being cursed," he called to them. "But she needs help. She's sick or something. Please, if there's anything you can do to help..." His words died on lips as they disappeared beneath the surface.

Moments later hands rose in the shallows, waiting for him to hand over the most precious person in his life. With a deep breath, he laid her in the water in their grasp. His heart thundered in his chest as Grae drifted out of his grip. When she submerged, his stomach roiled.

Elms and Simon grabbed his arms before he could charge into the water.

"Let them work," Elms scolded. "Trust them. She's theirs as much as yours." She pulled on his arm until his eyes met hers. "Let me take a look at that gash on you." Without her saying a word, Simon flicked on the flashlight feature of his smartphone so she could examine him in the darkness. "Hmm, looks like he only grazed you. We could glue it."

"Glue?"

"Yeah. It'll help keep it from bleeding too much. Head wounds can be a real bummer." She waved a hand at Simon and a tube of adhesive landed in her outstretched hand. "How'd he manage to get you? You're usually pretty quick with your changes."

"Yeah, well, I was a little distracted." Admitting he hadn't been listening for the gun wouldn't do anyone any good. He kept his mouth shut.

"Too distracted by your mate?" She singsonged, "Admit it."

"Where did she go?" Panic took over basic thoughts as he realized Grae was no longer visible.

"Trust them to care for her. She's one of them." Elms dabbed at the cut on his head with a swab before applying the glue by Simon's flashlight app. "Can you still feel her?"

He reached his telepathy as far and wide as he could until at the edge of his gift, a sweet voice called his name. Relief surged through his bloodstream when a dark head pushed through the surface of the water, and the sweet smile belonging only to Grae met his eyes.

∿∿

Watching Grae step from the lake's waters all on her own was a thing of haunting beauty. She looked every bit the woman he'd always known she would be. Empowered. Confident. Sexy. And the heated look in her gaze blazed a path across his skin as she eyed him up and down.

In his willingness to lose her, he'd gained so much more. Not just rights to her body and soul, but her love. She was as much a piece of him as the growing bulge in his pants.

His woman walked with the grace of a supermodel, her bared body glistening under the light of the moon and stars. He ached to run to her, wrap her in his arms and never let her loose. But his feet stayed rooted to the ground as his mouth went dry at the surge of adrenaline streaming through his blood. Transfixed, he counted every second it took for her to close the gap between them. Thirteen. Fourteen endless seconds until her hands slid into his hair. Fifteen pained seconds before she rose to her tiptoes. Sixteen fucking seconds before her lips caressed his.

The world rushed into present time as the spell holding him back broke. His hands itched to touch her everywhere at once and ensure she was whole. Her slick skin brushed against the solid pane of his chest, and she shivered.

"Let's get you out of here." The huskiness in his voice betrayed the thoughts streaming through his head.

"Let's," she agreed, a twinkle in her eye. She stepped back and laced a hand into his.

"That's our cue to leave." Elms placed her arm in Simon's, and the couple strode off without looking back.

Charlie waited until he heard their car start, his eyes never leaving Grae's. "Allow me," he finally offered and plucked her into his arms, carrying her through the trees to where his truck was parked on the road. "No reason to get your feet all cut up." He set her down on the passenger side and grabbed the duffel from the floorboards before allowing her entry into the cab. "I brought a few things."

Before handing over the bag, he looked his fill, his aim to memorize every detail and inch of her skin. Surely, other nights of bared flesh beneath the moon lurked in their future, but this one would always hold a special place in his heart. This night began the rest of their lives. This moment would disappear as soon as she placed his clothes on her body and hopped into his truck.

As if hearing every thought in his mind, Grae took half a step back and raised her hands to her sides. "This is all I have to offer you, Charlie Latham. My heart. My soul. My body. It's yours if you want it. All I ask in return is nothing less of you." She clasped her hands together at her breast and tilted her head while she waited.

"You've always had me, Grae, even when you didn't know it." He added one of his hands to her clasped hands.

"Are you still afraid of the bond? I promise not to abandon you," she added without an ounce of hesitation.

"I almost lost you too many times in the last twenty-four hours to let fear rule my heart anymore."

"Good," she whispered, pulling him close. "Then take me home, love. We have years to make up for."

He smiled at the innuendo. "Put on some clothes, Grae, or I'm not sure I can be held responsible for what happens next."

"By chance would it be something fun in the back of the truck?" The playful look on her face said everything her words didn't.

"Hell, yes." The words rumbled in his chest as the urge to throw her over his shoulder and make good on the fantasy warred with his good sense.

"Good. I've been dying to see if you're as handsome under the stars as you are under the shower spray."

No further words were exchanged. Every male hormone in his body formed a mosh pit in his pants. He bit back the temptation to take her right there, on the side of the road, up against the side of the cab. Instead, he made good on his promise.

The bed liner wasn't the most comfortable surface to slide skin against, but the emergency kit in the backseat included a small blanket for stranded drivers in the winter. It'd do nicely to protect her delicate skin. "Stay," he growled as he pawed through the kit until his hands touched fleece.

The blanket was launched over the side of the truck bed an instant before Grae was carefully lifted over. "Lie down," he ordered after smoothing the material. "I need to taste every damn inch of you."

The smile she gave before she complied with his haughty demand made the last semblances of sanity drift away. No sooner had her ass landed on the blanket, than he jumped the side of the truck and kneeled at her feet. He craved the taste of her against his lips. The sweet scent of her arousal tickled his nose and drove his ache to new heights. With no clothes to impede his progress, he went straight for the delicate curve of her ankle. He laved his tongue over first one, then the other, before moving up the muscular line of her calves.

A moan echoed in his ears as he found the sensitive spot behind her knee. His lips grazed and snacked, while his fingers played along the soft skin of her other leg. A whimper soon followed, Grae's breath coming in short bursts.

"Please," she begged as her fingertips gripped his hair and gently pulled.

"Please, what?" he teased with feigned ignorance.

"Please," she moaned, words seemingly alluding her.

With a broad smile, he widened her legs and slid his shoulders beneath them. Hands at her core, he opened her to his mouth and savored the first blissful lick. Sweeter than honey, and as ready as he himself was. His restraint faltered.

Gone were the slow, torturous kisses and swirls of his tongue, instead they were replaced by insistent and pointed darting to the sweet spot, as his fingers delved deep into her warmth, stroking and coaxing her release. Her thighs closed around his head as her muscles tightened. Back arching, his name found life from her lips and drove him mad with need.

Again. He needed to hear her call his name again. His planted a soft kiss on the inside of one thigh, then scraped his teeth against the skin of the other before moving to her stomach and up farther, until her breasts were his for the ravishing.

The material of his jeans was too much. Her heat pulsed against his zipper, and his cock begged for release. A quick nibble on her breast sent her writhing against him, wanton and needing. He abandoned her breast for the sweet curve of her neck and marked it his property before soothing the ache with long strokes. A gentle kiss on her temple did little to calm the rocking of her hips against his.

"Pleasssssssssse," she panted, her head thrashing from side to side as her fingers dug into his denim-covered backside, anchoring him where she wanted.

He sat back on his heels, the empty air between them cold. "I can't refuse you, Grae. Not now, not ever." Nimble fingers made quick work of shedding his jeans and hoodie. Before he could dip down to her level, Grae was on her knees, his hardened cock in her hand.

"My turn," she breathed. With a nod of her head, she directed him to the now vacant blanket.

Propped on elbows, he enjoyed the visual feast before him. She licked her lips, a quick dart of her tongue against the ruby buds, before she wrapped them around the head of his shaft. He swallowed a groan as she slid her mouth as far as she could along his skin. Her hands covered the skin her mouth missed. His eyes refused to close as a curtain of her long hair shielded her face from his view. The need coursing through him threatened to overtake the tenuous grip he had on his control. He needed to claim her. Make her his again. Prove to her she would never be satisfied by another.

Before he could make the move, Grae pushed an index finger into his chest and let his cock spring from her warm mouth.

"Lie down."

His own command echoing from her lips drove him mad, but he complied without hesitation. Her hair danced on the night breeze as she positioned herself over his erection and ran her hands up her rib cage, her back arched and her head thrown back. Goddess was the word that came to mind. And she was all his.

Unable to refrain any longer, he grabbed her hips and joined them with one well-aimed thrust. The mutual sighs of satisfaction drove him until she took control of the angle and pace. Slow. Precise. Sweet torture.

Her hands danced up his stomach and played across his chest, as his own hands dug into the flesh covering her hips. Their mating was as much an act of passion as it was a claiming; a promise.

By the time they lay spent on the blanket, sated and happy, he knew forever with Grae would be too short.

He kissed her temple and pulled her tight against his side. "Make an honest man of me."

"I don't know about all that," she teased as her fingers circled his nipple in lazy strokes, coaxing the heat to rise again.

"Grae," he warned.

"Will you be able to stop drinking that awful tea if I do?"

Laughing, he agreed.

"Good. The smell of that stuff makes my nose itch." She winked. "I'd be honored to be yours forever, Charlie Latham."

"Good. Because I have plans for the rest of my life, and each one includes you."

Epilogue

Shared Random Thought # 1 - The first day of the rest of your life only matters if it's shared with those you love.

Colin and Simon built the altar around an old bit of stone foundation, while Callie bustled about with a smoking batch of sage. Elms' approval of the smudging left a lasting smile on the witch's face as she worked. Charlie sank his heels into the soft earth and willed himself centered. Here he was. Doing the one thing he swore he'd never do. And damn if it didn't seem like the best idea ever. His knuckles popped as his fists clenched and relaxed in rhythmic fashion.

"She's almost ready."

Elms' hand landed on his arm and pulled him from his thoughts. He forced his body not to recoil under her touch. Damn. Turning back now was not an option. He'd not only created the bond between himself and Grae, but he'd almost lost her when he'd turned and ran like the chicken shit he was. His heart thundered in his chest and the sky above darkened.

"Stop it, Charlie. Don't doubt yourself now. She needs you. Be strong." Elms glared at him as if she could read the thoughts running a mile a minute through his brain.

Arguing with the stubborn healer was not an option. He knew her fiery husband's nature was calm and collected unless she got riled up, and he didn't want to deal with Simon today too.

"Yeah, yeah. I'm trying." He rolled his head and cracked his neck. "I swore I'd never mate." The words were meant for Elms, but he wasn't really talking to her, he was talking more to himself. "When my mom died, I watched my father deteriorate into a shell of the man he'd been. He drank himself into oblivion and wrapped his truck around the biggest damn tree he

253

could find." He kicked the toe of his shoe into the ground, refusing to meet Elms' eyes. He could hear the thoughts in her head and he didn't dare look up to witness the pity on her face. "Look, Grae and I've been doing this dance since we were young. I always knew she would be perfect for me deep down. But I already almost lost her, Elms. How the hell do I keep her safe?"

Oh, Charlie. You have always been my most ardent protector. You are my safe haven. My shelter in a storm. My light in the darkness. My home.

Grae's voice wafted through his in the musical tone his body craved, and it softened the worry in his chest.

"I can see you've figured it out," Elms teased. "Tell Gracie it's almost time." She added a wink before turning back toward Colin and Simon.

Elms wants you to be on time.

Grae's resulting chuckle over their mental pathway warmed his heart. *Are you afraid, Mr. Latham?*

Of what?

Another burst of her sweet laughter, but this time it came from behind him. Her breath tickled his neck and her lips caressed his skin, teeth gently scraping as they went.

"That I'd change my mind? Run now, while there's still time?" She nipped his earlobe, then swirled her tongue over the mark.

Their hearts beat in unison in his head. Eager. Excited. Energized for what came next.

"You know I'm only doing this for you," he grumbled, biting back a smile.

"Oh, really?"

Her hands slid under the tails of his shirt and made their way up his chest. Sparks of fire blazed in the wake of her every caress. She knew him better than he knew himself, and rather than annoy him, it made him want to grab her, yell "I do," and take her home to their future.

"I like the way you think," she purred. "Let's go make it official."

Her fingers playfully pinched his skin before the heat of her disappeared. Charlie wanted to hold firm and not steal a glance at his bride-to-be, but he couldn't resist a quick peek. Hot damn. The back of the dress was held together with thin strips of fabric, crisscrossing her back like a present waiting to be unwrapped, while her bare skin lay smooth beneath. His fingers begged to reach for her, but *tsk-tsk* wafted through his brain.

"Grae," he rumbled in warning. "I thought you wanted to make it to the altar today?"

"I do," she called over her shoulder with a laugh. "But I want you to eat your heart out on the way."

He could imagine the smirk on her face, and it made him laugh. She was perfect for him. Completely and irrevocably perfect.

Charlie stood beside Colin on his side of the make-shift altar, unsure how to remove his jaw from the ground. Grae looked stunning in her gown. The top resembled a corset from the front, and the skirt flowed like a river in great waves of fabric tumbling to the ground. She was a dream. No. She was *his* dream. Her eyes lit up when her mind heard his declaration of approval.

As promised, Simon kept the ceremony short and sweet. Grae's "I do" was out of her mouth before Simon finished asking her the question, to their friends' delight. Charlie only let a beat pass before adding his "I do" before Simon even had a chance to speak again. With the echo of laughter in his ears, he reached for his wife and pulled her against his chest. She smelled of cinnamon and vanilla, spicy and warm. Heaven.

He took his time weaving a hand into her hair and pulling her closer. Kissing her wasn't for show, despite the audience. It was deep, passionate, and filled with his longing.

"I guess this is where I pronounce them husband and wife, so long as no one objects," Simon called over the hoots and hollers.

Unable to wait much longer to officially consummate their human marriage, Charlie gathered Grae into his arms and lifted her off her feet.

"Take me home?"

"Always," he promised, before tossing her over his shoulder and placing a hand on her ass. "You'll be coming home with me for the rest of forever."

THE END

Acknowledgements

With each book I worry I'll inevitably forget to thank someone, but once again, I'll do my best.

Thank you to my CRW, RWA, FF&P, and NJRW friends. Your inspiration is limitless.

Thank you to my friends and family—the list being longer than my body. You all know who you are and how much I love you, especially my kids who still believe I can do it all.

Thanks to Lara Stokes and Melissa Shank for beta reading, critiquing, and believing in me. You ladies are my foundation. I always know you have my six and are only a few taps of my fingers away. I love you ladies!

Thanks to Michelle Fairbanks for another fabulous cover. You captured the essence of the story with your art.

Thanks to my amazing editor from CMWAS.com, Gina Wynn. Charlie is a great book boyfriend thanks to you.

A huge thank you shout out to the members of "Jeni's Little Devils." This amazing group of readers keeps me working.

WIND'S SOLACE

A special thanks to Ryan Blauvelt for his on-the-spot knowledge of tornados and other fun facts that kept me writing instead of researching. Your help was greatly appreciated. I look forward to many more such conversations.

Also, a note of thanks to Jen Anderson, Vickie Rush, Brenda Onley, Jamie Pejo, Sophia Henry, and Tara Goodfellow for being the best "super fans" a girl could ask for!!

With all my love and thanks,

~ j

Did you enjoy this book?

If you enjoyed Wind's Solace, join Jeni's newsletter to get information about upcoming releases and giveaways.

Join Jeni's newsletter here: http://eepurl.com/cyxSTf
Jeni loves hearing from her readers, feel free to drop her a line, writer her a review, or connect with her on Facebook, Twitter, Goodreads, Pinterest, Instagram. You'll see just how much decaf she drinks and learn all about upcoming projects.

Visit www.jeniburns.com for upcoming announcements and book release information.

ABOUT THE AUTHOR

Jeni Burns is a Jersey Girl through and through, regardless where her mail is delivered. She lives in and is renovating an old Colonial with her two kids and one massive, bed-hogging, poodle.

Amidst all the chaos, she squirrels away in her office with her giant cup of decaf, a handful of Swedish Fish, and writes until the natives get restless and drag her back to reality.